Mrs. Daniel

Tried in the Fire

A tale: In three volumes. Vol. 3

Mrs. Daniel

Tried in the Fire
A tale: In three volumes. Vol. 3

ISBN/EAN: 9783337344597

Printed in Europe, USA, Canada, Australia, Japan

Cover: Foto ©Andreas Hilbeck / pixelio.de

More available books at **www.hansebooks.com**

TRIED IN THE FIRE.

A Tale.

BY

MRS. MACKENZIE DANIELS,

AUTHOR OF "MY SISTER MINNIE," "THE OLD MAID OF
THE FAMILY," "OUR GUARDIAN," "RUTH EARNLEY,"
ETC., ETC.

IN THREE VOLUMES.

VOL. III.

LONDON:
THOMAS CAUTLEY NEWBY, PUBLISHER,
30, WELBECK STREET CAVENDISH SQUARE.
1860.

TRIED IN THE FIRE.

CHAPTER I.

" Why don't you talk, Nelly ?—Say just what‚ ever you like—rail at them, and abuse them all to your heart's content. I deliver up the whole company of my amiable relatives to your tender mercies, only don't persist in this un- natural and painful silence, as if *I* were the person who had offended you."

They were at breakfast together, the morning succeeding the unpleasant visit in Park Lane ; and Ellen, looking pale, and decidedly out of temper, had hitherto replied in monosyllables to everything her husband had said to her.

"I am sorry to be disagreeable, Sydney," she answered, now really trying to put on a less gloomy expression, " but what is the good of talking? We are neither of us disposed to discuss indifferent matters, and I believe we have already said all that *can* be said on the painful subject engrossing the thoughts of both. When a thing is inevitable, the best way is to endure it philosophically."

" My poor Nelly, you are a bad specimen of a philosopher, I must confess; and unfortunately I am not in a position to be able to console you. I feel very like a man who is going to be hanged this morning; and upon my word, if it were not for all the trouble my uncle has taken about this con——, no, no, don't look so frightened, I won't swear, but about this anything but tempting situation, I would decline it even now."

"Impossible! we cannot continue living upon charity. I would rather become a public singer to-morrow. Indeed I should like to work."

"Nonsense, Ellen! you know I would sooner die than let you do such a thing. It isn't the work I care for. It is leaving you that cuts me up so; and you know it, little cruel icicle, though you are."

"Take me with you then."

"Only let me have a chance; but no, they have made up their minds that I shall go alone; they would say that I risked your life, and the child's, for my own selfish gratification. My own Nelly, we *must* endure it, miserable and terrible as it is."

"For me a thousand times more so than for

you.   Imagine having to bear for two long years that which, to escape for two months, induced me to consent to a secret marriage, and thus deprive myself of the little chance I ever should have had, of being respected in your proud and prejudiced family.   These are not lively reflections, are they, Sydney?"

"No, my darling, but you are perfectly certain, that I will not accede to any plan, however desirable it may seem, that is disagreeable to you.   I told you so last night."

"I know, but what can you do?—What can either of us do, to resist such a tide as the one setting against us? I suppose it is destiny; so let things take their course.   What can you say to people who declare that a wife would be disgracing her husband and her husband's family, by living in a house with her own mother!"

"Oh, but who thinks of even listening to such nonsense as this? I shall talk to my uncle about it, to-day; he, at least, is not unreasonable; and you know how fond he is of you, Nelly."

"He is always very kind, and for his sake I would not appear obstinate or ungrateful; but to live with Katherine, to be a poor relation in *that* house! Well, well, my philosophy is scarcely waterproof, it seems; so let us have done with the subject. And look, Sydney, it is nearly nine now; and you are to be there by half past."

"I am off then, but how will you kill time in my absence? I am so afraid you will get low-spirited and cry, poor darling little Nelly!— You are quite decided not to go to my mother?"

"Quite. I am not accustomed to such invitations as the one she gave me."

"Will you amuse yourself by writing to your brother, or to Norah Kennedy?"

"No. They will hear of my trouble soon enough. Don't be anxious about me, dear Sydney. Perhaps mamma will come; and in any case, I have always my little May, who will afford me as much consolation as I am capable of receiving. Good-bye, love; and mind you keep up your own spirits."

"Heaven bless you, my dearest!" he said, as he pressed her to his heart; and then, with a gentle kiss on the forehead of the sleeping baby, ran down the garden to stop the omnibus that was just passing their gate.

* * * * *

Ellen had spent the long morning in wandering restlessly about the house, carrying May, who was unusually fretful, in her arms, and trying to reason herself into a patient endurance of the evils her hasty and ill-advised marriage had so soon entailed upon her. Now that there was to be a sudden and complete breaking up of all, the last eleven months appeared like a dream to her—that gradually-accepted state of things, which she had believed to be her life's established destiny, was only then a brief episode of that life, to be succeeded by—what?

Ah, there was the question! Ellen's troubled thoughts could go no further than her domiciliation beneath the roof of Katherine Wilmot. This of itself seemed to comprehend whatever of gloomy and wretched, fate had it in its power to inflict.

Much as she would have dreaded the dangers and sufferings of a long sea-voyage, and the influence of a doubtful climate upon her baby's health, she would rather have accompanied her husband, had a choice been given her, than remained behind, to live with the Wilmots; but, as she had said to Sydney in the morning, what was to be done?

The family had settled it all their own way.

And though poor Ellen might fret and chafe, and even express freely, in private, her indignation and disgust at the tyranny exercised over her, she was quite aware that neither her circumstances nor constitutional tendencies would enable her finally to get the better of any strong will that opposed itself to her own.

She might certainly enlist her mother and

brother on her side ; but then Ellen's earnest desire was that neither of them should ever know how much reason she had to regret her marriage, or to dislike her husband's family.

Even amidst all their recent troubles, Mrs. Clavering had only heard that they were indebted to Mr. Wilmot for the payment of a heavy bill ; and that this gentleman was exerting himself to procure a government appointment for Sydney.

Ellen was not selfish in things of this nature, and perhaps, too, her pride might have influenced her a little in withholding from all her friends the painful facts that have been laid before the reader.

Even Norah, the confidante of every girlish care and anxiety, had not the faintest suspicion of what was going on ; and concluded, by not hearing from Ellen, that she was too happy and busy in her new maternal duties, to have any inclination for letter-writing.

"Two letters, ma'am!" said the servant, suddenly entering the parlour where her young mistress had at length settled herself with a view of coaxing baby to go to sleep. " Shall I take little missy, while you read them ?"

"Thank you! if you are not too busy down stairs, I shall be glad to be relieved for a short time, she has been so wakeful and cross all the morning."

" It's the teeth, ma'am, otherwise there never was a sweeter-tempered baby—but you look tired to death yourself. Better lie down for an' hour, and I'll see that nobody disturbs you."

"Oh, I shall not sleep, Mary, but I will rest on the sofa while you keep May. If anybody calls, however, I *must* receive them. Mr. Willand expects several persons on business."

The girl retired with her charge, and Ellen opened her letters, both of which had arrived by the twopenny post.

The first was from her mother, and only contained a few affectionate enquiries after her own and baby's health, and a promise of coming to tea on the following day.

The second was from Gertrude Lomond, and terminated thus—

" You will be agreeably surprised, I think, to hear of a rencontre I had yesterday. Walking along Oxford Street very quickly, for I had come into town solely on business, I was suddenly arrested by a pale, tall lady, who, holding out her hand with a smile, exclaimed, ' I hope I see Miss Gertrude well.' A second glance brought back my scattered faculties, and I recognized the Mrs. Lane who spent one summer at Madame Guillemar's, and who took such a

particular fancy to you. Of course you were
the chief topic of our hurried conversation, and
it ended in my giving her your address, and her
promising to call on you the very first day she
was able to get so far. You may, therefore, expect her at any minute ; and I thought I would
write to tell you of it, as you may like to remain
at home until after her visit. I remember what
great friends you were, &c. &c."

There had been a time, and not so very long
ago, when nothing would have afforded Ellen
Clavering greater pleasure than a renewal of her
acquaintance with the good and pious Mrs.
Lane ; but Ellen Willand was altogether a different person, (at least she felt so herself), and
the thought of an immediate visit from her
former friend, did not give her the gratification
it certainly ought to have done.

And this, not in reference to her temporal

prospects and circumstances, (for Ellen knew that she was not obliged to enter upon these), but having to do with that inner, spiritual life, concerning which she doubted not Mrs. Lane would frankly and fully question her.

For when they had parted about four years previous to the present time, the young school-girl had given some evidence of having had her heart touched by the living fire, and the long tried and experienced Christian woman had hoped the best things of one who had ap- • parently been so much in earnest, and whose natural disposition was too open and candid for feigning of any sort.

And now they were to meet again.

Sooner, too, than even Ellen anticipated ; for, while she was in the midst of all the sad and depressing thoughts the recollection of this early friend had called into existence, and which, for the time, entirely put to flight the more positive troubles by which she was surrounded, the garden bell tinkled gently, and, running to the window, Ellen saw Mrs. Lane coming up the pathway to the house.

CHAPTER II.

THE interview was a long one, and to Ellen, at least, fraught with much agitation and excitement, for, as she had anticipated, Mrs. Lane spoke to her freely on those subjects which, for so many months, she had banished altogether from her thoughts ; and, instead of calming, as it would have done had her religion grown into a reality, it only added to the fever and disquiet of her mind, and made her a great deal more unhappy than she had been before.

Ellen did not, however, for a moment seek to

deceive the friend who evinced so strong and earnest an interest in her highest welfare. If possible, she even exaggerated her own sins and short-comings, and Mrs. Lane, in her turn, did not disguise that she mourned over the failure of her hopes concerning one to whom she had so warmly attached herself, as a mother mourns over a child who has disappointed her most sanguine expectations.

" I will see you again, my dear," she said, at parting, " if my visits and faithful speaking are not repugnant to you ; and be assured that you will never be forgotten when I am praying for those most dear to me. I believe, firmly believe, Ellen, that you will have a rough and thorny path to tread, for whom the Lord loveth He chasteneth ; and has He not already given some proofs of loving you ? but God alone knows how much they lose who do not serve

Him in their *youth*, as I thought and hoped once, you would have done. Let me kiss your little child again, that its image may live beside your own in my heart. And now, farewell, and may Israel's God, who knows how to win and keep all who are His, be with you for evermore."

She was gone, and poor Ellen, with flushed cheeks and throbbing temples, could only lie down on the sofa from which she had risen hastily on her visitor's arrival, and cry till Sydney came home.

Then the instinct which told her that he could by no possibility sympathize with her present grief, made her quickly dash away all traces of the tears, and meet him with as much semblance of cheerfulness as she could, on so brief a notice, assume.

Contrary to his wont, however, and, indeed

to all his wife's previous experience of him, Sydney was looking gloomy and discontented; and, for a long time, would only reply in the shortest and driest sentences to the questions she asked him.

Her own preoccupation of mind caused Ellen to be slower in perceiving this than she might otherwise have been; but at last it forced itself upon her observation, and then she said, very naturally, and speaking with her usual good temper—

" What is the matter, Sydney ?" He was about to answer " nothing," as is the usual habit with husbands—sometimes even with wives—on these sort of occasions, but dissimulation and crossness to his wife were alike new to Sydney; and suddenly dashing down a parcel he had been holding in his hand, (as a relief, probably,

to his overburdened feelings,) he exclaimed im-
petuously,—

"Hang it all! I should have thought it was
enough to be obliged to go and live amongst
those Hottentots out there, without having
it dinned into my ears that my wife is glad to-
get rid of me.   A man isn't allowed a chance·
of making himself happy anyhow."

"What is all this, Sydney dear?" asked
Ellen, turning a little pale; "who has dared
to assert that your wife is glad to get rid of
you?"

"Oh, nobody has exactly asserted it," he
replied more mildly, for her tone of voice seemed to reassure him, "but Katherine hinted as
much; and though I didn't believe her, Nelly,
you see, darling, it made me feel queer and
savage with all the world.   Come and kiss me,
and tell me you forgive my ill-temper.   Poor

ittle woman! as if you had not enough without this."

"That wicked girl!" said Ellen, passionately; " but now what can be her motive? I hope you told her it was untrue."

" To be sure I did; but she smiled in her sardonic way, and said she was glad I had so much confidence, &c., &c. I should explain, however, that it all arose out of my trying to convince them that it would be better for you to live with your mother, in my absence—you see I didn't forget you, Nelly."

"Thank you dear, and what further objections did they make?"

" Oh, they brought forward all sorts of ridiculous arguments against it; and Kate, in particular, pretended that once in your own family again, you would not care for my coming back; that your brother, being a Methodist, would convince you there was danger in living with a worldly husband; that you would infallibly become a Methodist yourself, having been inclined that way even at school; and, in short, they talked me into a downright passion, and I believe I abused them all, except my uncle, who tried in vain, to make the women hold their tongues."

"Poor dear Sydney! what a morning you must have had! and all for nothing, it seems, since the plans remain as they stood last night; . is it not so?"

"Oh, as far as *their* wishes are concerned, yes, but we are not bound to obey them like slaves. I don't believe you would have a moment's peace with Katherine, and we will see what other arrangement can be made."

"No, love," said Ellen, laying her hand on her husband's arm, and speaking very firmly,—

"let us give in to them for this once. It will not be for long; and I promise you that if I find it too uncomfortable, I will leave and go to mamma."

Her morning's meditations and interview with Mrs. Lane had made her almost indifferent, for the time, as to the temporal position in which she was to be placed.

" Very well, my dearest, have it all your own way. No doubt the air of the Highlands would brighten up our little snowdrop, if you could really bear it for a month or two."

" Of course I can ; but they will not, I suppose, be going to Scotland till the Autumn."

"No, and in the meanwhile there can be no reason why you should not stay with your mother if you like it, or take a trip to St. Ives. I will trust you, Nelly, even with that fascinating guardian, just to show you how little I heed Kate's insinuations."

" Oh," said Ellen, with a passing smile— " John Arnold is anything but fascinating, Sydney."

" What is he then, since I am sure you think a great deal of him ?"

" He is only a good man," she replied instinctively using the words with which she was accustomed to associate him in her own mind.

" I am afraid that is more than you would say of me, Nelly, though it sounds like particularly commonplace praise ;—will you go, though, when I leave you, and stay awhile with Grace Arnold ?"

"I don't think so," Ellen replied, " but you must not take this for a final answer. I shall feel so utterly desolate when you are gone, (though at present I cannot in the least realize it), that there is no saying what I may be induced to do."

"Poor dear little wifey! I know you will feel dull. It breaks my heart to think of leaving you. I don't believe that anybody, not even your own mother, will care for you, and pet you as I have done."

"That is very, very true, Sydney, but don't let us talk about it now, I am so miserably low to-day. What is that small parcel you threw on the ground, with such fierce indignation, awhile ago?"

"Oh," he said, stooping to pick it up, "there's not much in it, Nelly, only a couple of pair of gloves, and a little scarf that I bought for you in Regent Street. My uncle gave me a cheque, (which, of course, I shall pay him again the moment my salary begins), to get some kind of an outfit, and I could not have money in my pocket without thinking of the little woman at home. Look, are these the colours you like?"

"Oh Sydney," she replied, with tears in her eyes, "you are really too good to me. And you could go and buy me these things, even after the cruelties your cousin had been saying!"

"Of course I could, my Nelly; I should not love you less if I knew for certainty that you did not care one straw for me. I do not understand *that* affection which is dependent upon the return it gets."

"Ah well—you deserve a better wife than I have been, Sydney—but we must positively think a little about buisiness now. Have you a list of what you will require for your outfit?"

" Yes, and my uncle is of opinion that you had better get the things as soon as possible. We will go out together to-morrow, if you like."

" Alone, I hope?"

"Oh yes—my mother hinted something about accompanying us, but I told her plainly there was no need for it. I am quite resolved to have you all to myself these last few weeks."

Alas! how quickly those last few weeks went by—how soon it came to the last few days, and then the last few hours! Both the husband and wife had spoken much when they were together (and Sydney contrived that they should be nearly always together now) of the bitter pain they should suffer in parting, but neither of them at all understood *what* it would be, because they had had no actual experience of this sort of thing.

*   *   *   *   *

"Upon my soul, Nelly, you must try not to look in that way, or if I'm to be hacked to pieces the next moment, I cannot and will not leave you."

They had just sat down to their last meal together—not to eat, you may be very sure—when Sydney thus addressed his wife, whose colourless face and quivering lips (to say nothing of the fixed sadness in her usually sunny eyes) certainly justified in some degree this affectionate remonstrance.

"Don't notice me, then," she replied, swallowing a cup of nearly boiling tea to drown the rising hysteria in her throat. "I am doing my best, Sydney; and I daresay I look worse than I feel."

"I wish I could think so, my darling. I would rather, now it has come to this, believe Katherine's assertions—mad as they made me at the time—than know you were miserable after I am gone. I am selfish in everything but my love for you, Nelly."

The poor wife was fairly done for now, and clinging to her husband, who had sprung towards her at the first sight of her tears, she sobbed as if her heart were really breaking.

" Nelly, Nelly, my own, my darling—do you know that you are killing me by this grief?"

More sobs, more torrents of burning tears, and then more passionate, imploring entreaties, from the no less wretched and agitated husband, that she would be calm and quiet for *his* sake.

So they went on, for nearly half an hour, which brought it very close to the time when the cab was to be at the door, to take him away altogether.

Fortunately for both of them, Nurse now came in with little May, whe had only just awoke.

The woman saw what was taking place, and, without a word, she put the child into its father's arms, and went out of the room again.

"Poor little lady!" said Sydney, hastily brushing aside either his own tears or those that his wife had left on his face, "she is happily unconscious of all *our* sorrow, Nelly. Look, she is actually laughing, as if it was a very merry scene she had been brought in to witness. Stony-hearted May—you don't deserve that I should waste one of these precious moments upon you." .

But Nelly took advantage of the baby's arrival to run to her own room, and dip her burning face and eyes in cold, fresh water, that she might, at the very last moment, sustain, if possible, her husband's courage, by appearing to have regained composure herself.

He had all along set her the example of such entire unselfishness.

When she returned to the parlour, May was in her cradle, and the young father kneeling beside it, looking very, very grave and sad—and as if—were this scene to be prolonged—he could not, with all his courage, endure it.

The sound of wheels was suddenly heard by them both; and Ellen ran to the window to conceal her excessive trembling.

"Is everything ready?" asked Sydney, hoping to turn her attention to common-place things, and thus prevent another distressing scene before the servants.

"Yes—everything," she replied in a voice whose unnatural calmness could not deceive him. "Mary has just taken the last few small packages that remained, into the hall. Your over-coat and hat are here."

"Ah, there is the gate bell, and the man is

rather late, I believe. Well, I must say good bye, you know—This is hard work, Nelly."

"Kiss baby first—poor baby—you know I shall take care of her."

"And of yourself too, I hope. There, there, I have nearly smothered her small ladyship, and she is thinking seriously of having a good cry at last. God bless her—God bless and preserve my little fragile daughter. And now, Nelly, my wife, my dearest of all, come to me."

One long, silent, tearless embrace—a few confused and broken words—an interchange of looks that spoke more of the heart's utter misery than either of them had ever ventured with their lips to utter—and then came the inevitable moment.

And that dreaded and dreadful parting, between the young husband and the young wife, was over.

CHAPTER III.

DESOLATE indeed!

She had said that it would be so, but her very gloomiest imaginings on the subject had never at all approached the sad, sad reality.

She never guessed, until her husband was actually gone, how completely his devotion and tenderness had grown into a necessity of her life.

But now she felt it.

Mrs. Clavering came and took her away from the cottage a few hours after Sydney's departure; but although the sympathizing mother was kindness and patience itself, and little Mrs. Miniver did everything in her power to raise the spirits, and excite the interest, of the poor wife who had become her guest, it was all insufficient to dispel the settled melancholy that had taken possession of her; and so, at length, without even consulting her on the subject, Mrs. Clavering wrote to Maurice to get a short holiday, and come and take his sister and her baby to the Arnolds, who had sent Ellen repeated invitations, and would be really delighted to have her.

It was a happy thought on the mother's part, for the brother and sister had not met since the marriage of the latter, and on his unannounced appearance one fine summer evening amongst them, Ellen uttered an exclamation of such joyful and animated surprise, that Mrs. Clavering secretly applauded her own wisdom, and felt convinced that her scheme would answer excellently.

At first, however, Ellen strongly opposed the suggestion of so long a journey. She was not in good health; she should be a most stupid companion for Gracie; she did not like to trouble them with the baby, &c. &c.

But Maurice, who was of course enchanted, on his own account, at the prospect of a visit to St. Ives, patiently combated all these objections, and succeeded, in the end, in persuading Ellen that it was her duty to yield to their wishes.

In truth he had been greatly shocked at the alteration he perceived in his sister; and it was very natural that he should think nobody could do her so much good as his gentle little Gracie.

"And as for John," he had said, "you will see scarcely anything of him; for he has more work to do than ever; and Gracie writes me word that she is almost always alone."

So they went.

The first sight of the village, and of all the old, familiar faces and objects, excited a whole tumult of emotions in Ellen's mind; and after having been moderately cheerful, and certainly quite composed, during the journey, she gave way, and cried like a child now that its termination approached.

"Never mind, dear—it will do you good," said Maurice, affectionately, as she was trying to apologize for her stupidity—"and nothing, I am sure, can be more natural. Our friends will understand and sympathize with you."

They did indeed; welcoming her and her little one with the warmest expressions of pleasure and satisfaction, and making her comprehend at once that while she would be treated as an esteemed and honoured guest, she would be permitted the still greater privilege of feeling herself perfectly at home.

" And yet here, even here, Ellen knew that she was not a first object—that their interest in her—true and affectionate as she felt it to be—was only a reflected one, bestowed upon Maurice's sister, and warmed into an active, instead of a passive sentiment, by the goodness and benevolence of their own hearts.

Alas! even here she was to miss her husband's exclusive love, and to be oppressed by a vain and yearning regret for that which had never been appreciated till it was lost.

The Arnolds thought her very much changed in every way, but she had a stronger claim upon them in her sorrow and desolation, than she had had in the midst of her girlhood's brightest and happiest moments.

Ellen herself had no idea how much and often she was talked of by this quiet brother and sister, nor how they mourned over the marriage which, in separating her from them, had hitherto done so little in promoting her individual happiness.

Maurice could only stay a very few days at St. Ives, so, of course, they left him as much as possible to Gracie, and during this brief period, Ellen was not unfrequently consigned to the companionship of John Arnold, who, in consideration of his friend's visit, managed to be more at home while it lasted, than on ordinary occasions.

It did her good in many ways. Chiefly by giving her, as a constant study, a human heart living out of itself and its own personal cares— living in and for the interests, the hopes, the sufferings, and the necessities, both temporal and spiritual, of others.

It was a healthy life, a pure life, a life that even without its deeper, diviner signification, would have been a beautiful and admirable thing —a lesson to any who might be privileged to watch its daily, noiseless, unobtrusive course—a course that Ellen knew would brighten and brighten, (in spite of all the earthly clouds and damps that must surround it) until it reached the perfect day.

And so it did her good to observe and think about it now, and to contrast it with her own wasted, profitless existence, which indeed was always rising up like a threatening ghost before her mental vision, and interfering sadly with the very little comfort or happiness she could ever at this time be said to enjoy.

It was no slight trial to her to lose Maurice again so soon, but he was obliged to go; and then the Arnolds fell into their usual very quiet, monotonous mode of life, to which Ellen gladly conformed, and summer shed its glories over the dear familiar scenes, and the little May grew stronger and lovelier every day; and in all the outward life of the mother there came a pleasant, soothing lull.

This went on for nearly six weeks, before the expiration of which Ellen was looking almost herself again, and beginning to feel more rationally happy and contented than she had done for a very considerable time.

Her correspondence with Norah Kennedy was now resumed, and this really devoted friend, who had as yet found nothing in life that interested her more warmly than Ellen and Ellen's destiny, rejoiced sincerely at the tone of her letters, and believed that she had emerged permanently from the shade, and would henceforth bask in an atmosphere of calm, genial sunshine.

This warm-hearted, but spiritually unen-lightened girl, never reflected that, even were such a condition possible, it would be the last in the world to be desired for a character like Ellen's.

And had Ellen herself for a few pleasant weeks been deluded into any such expecta-tion, it would have been entirely put to flight, when one morning, as she sat at breakfast with her friends, a letter was delivered to her from Mrs. Wilmot. For it stated that, in conse-quence of Katherine having been for some time far from well, the family had decided on going to Scotland at least a month earlier than they had originally intended; and they there-fore begged her to join them in London immediately. A few polite hopes that she had derived benefit from the country air, were added ; also Katherine's and Mr. Wilmot's kind regards; and so the letter concluded.

" Bad news, I am afraid, dear," said Gracie, who saw how pale Ellen had suddenly become ; " but it is not from your husband ?"

" Oh no, it is only from Mrs. Wilmot. They desire me to come to them immediately —they are going to Scotland."

" I am very sorry ; how provoking it is ; and you were getting so much better."

" Gracie," said her brother, " we must not make things appear worse to Ellen, by speaking of our own regrets.   She *must* know, without a word from us on the subject, how greatly we shall miss her."

The ready tears came into Ellen's eyes, and she would not trust herself to answer.

" But we were so happy and comfortable,"

urged poor Grace, who was not always quite so wise as John ; " I really cannot help saying how very, very disagreeable, this summons is to me."

" It can't be helped, however," exclaimed Ellen, in a trembling voice; " I shall have to start to-morrow morning, so you must help me pack to-day, Gracie."

" Ah, don't talk about it ; and John—(turning to her brother)—you will at least endeavour to be home early this afternoon. Ellen will like to see as much as she can of you, I know, although if we did not both understand you, we should think you did not care a bit about her going."

" You would think wrongly then," he replied, rising as he spoke. " I shall go out at once, that I may get back quickly. Keep up your courage, Ellen, and remember that this, and all things being appointed, *must* be right and wise. Good morning."

"Don't fancy he is cold or unfeeling," said Gracie, as her brother left the room ; " you know John never shows when he is sorry, but he can't deceive *me*, and you may be quite satisfied with the amount of his regret at losing you."

" Oh, I am," Ellen replied, with a faint smile ; " but, Gracie, if you only knew how I dread my life with these people !"

*   *   *   *

It was Ellen's own wish to have her luggage sent on, and to walk to the place from whence the coach would start on the following morning. The exercise would do her good, and the fresh air be better for baby, and more likely to make her sleep than a drive in a close carriage Grace said she would go too, and see the last of them ; but when the time came, she had one of her bad headaches, and could not even rise from the sofa.

So, after parting with many tears from her future sister, who was already as dear to her as if the ties of kindred united them, Ellen and John Arnold, followed by the nurse and baby, started on their early walk, which promised to be anything but a cheerful one.

He tried to make her talk, however, and, quite contrary to his usual habit, was very talkative himself, calling her attention to everything he thought likely to excite a passing interest, and doing all he possibly could to banish from his own mind, as well as hers, the fact that she was going hundreds and hundreds of miles away, and might never return to this quiet village again.

Ellen was the first to allude to it, but this

was not until she was just getting into the coach, and knew that in less than five minutes he would be gone. Then she said, making a great effort to speak calmly—

"I will not even attempt to thank you for all your kindness to me, nothing that I have ever experienced will live longer, as a precious memory, in my heart; and if we are not to meet again in this world (for who knows what may happen?), believe at least that I shall think of you while life endures with the deepest gratitude and respect. I never can forget you."

"May the Lord bless, and win, and guide you!" he said in reply, not even looking into those swimming blue eyes, that might perhaps have made him feel more human than he wished just then to feel. "And if ever in life's mysterious changes you should need either

a friend or a home, you will know where to
come—you will not hesitate, or doubt us ?"

"Never—how could I ?—Here, kiss my little
May—she will perhaps be a bonnie lassie before
you see her again."

He availed himself of this permission with
infinite gentleness, for he loved little children,
and this one above all others. Then, with
another hasty "God bless you both," in which
the man rather than the minister spoke, he
turned away and left them.

Immediately after, the noisy coach drove off;
and Ellen, leaning back in her corner, and cover-
ing her flushed face, saw the life to which she
was being whirled stretching out (like a chain of
dull, bleak hills, on a sunless day) before her.

CHAPTER IV.

ELLEN WILLAND TO NORAH KENNEDY.

"*The Glens, October 20th,* 18—.

"DEAREST NORAH,

"I can scarcely believe that I have been two months in this place, without writing you a single line; but your letter assures me of the fact, gently insinuating, at the same time, that you would avoid thinking me cold and indolent if you could help it; but you cannot help it— that is clear. And I have no spirit wherewith to vindicate myself. I would just as soon you thought the worst of me, for I have sufficient faith in you to feel assured that you will love me none the less. And now, enough on this subject, for I want to write you a long letter about other things ; and to-day is one of my *low* days, which *will* come, from time to time, although nothing is *so* bad here as I had anticipated — and it is in truth a lovely, lovely place !

" I have said that nothing is *so* bad as I had anticipated it would be. Of course I don't know what it may become ; for hitherto the house has been filled with company ever since our arrival, and nobody has had much time to notice me—poor, insignificant little me ! who thought once that wherever I went, love and admiration *must* accompany me—I am a bit wiser now, at all events about some things.

But I was going to tell you that Katherine has been ill, and in bad spirits, for I don't know how long ; and they have an idea that constant society, and plenty of it, is absolutely essential to her recovery. For my own part, I think differently ; but who would ever dream of asking the opinion of a poor and dependant connection of the family, which is what I am here, of course, as everybody, down to the lowest servant, knows !

" Well, in consequence of Katherine's myste- rious depression (I am afraid *I* can guess its source), we have a superabundance of gaiety— dinner-parties, balls, concerts, fêtes champetres, picnics up the beautiful lochs, and I don't know what besides.

" Except the concerts, at which my singing is required, I am allowed the privilege of declining to join in these festivities ; and I often gladly

avail myself of it, and spend the time of the
family's absence in wandering with my nurse
and baby amongst the wild and exquisite scenery
around the Glens.   This is real and intense en-
joyment to me, and while it lasts I forget all my
troubles—see no shadows in the future—see
nothing but the blue, sparklings lochs, the dark,
winding valleys, the heathery mountains, and the
pure, cloudless sky looking down so calmly upon
it all.

" Occasionally, Katherine makes one of her
old, sneering remarks upon my romantic tastes,
and observes, that it is a pity *you* are not here
to sentimentalize with me ; (she never by any
chance mentions my husband to me).   By the
bye, I ought to have told you before, that I have
had one long, delightful letter from Sydney, in
which he assures me he is quite well, and beginning to work very hard ; only that his home

is miserably dull without us—May and myself—
and that he has already pinned up over his bed
a paper, like schoolboys have, to notch off every
morning the day past, and which brings him
twenty-four hours nearer the time of our re-
union. Poor, dear Sydney! he cannot possibly
miss me more than I miss him. He was un-
wise to spoil me as he did.

"But I am always running away from what
I meant to tell you about Katherine. She has,
of course, a vast number of admirers, and I believe not a few offers, though nobody ever thinks
of speaking on family affairs to me. Amongst
the whole of her worshippers, there is only one
to whom she is even cordially polite, and he, I
fancy, ought scarcely to be called a worshipper,
notwithstanding that he is evidently a little flattered at being distinguished by a young lady who
is spoken of everywhere as a miracle of pride

E 2

and coldness. His name is Mervyn, and he is a widower, quite young though, and without children. I have heard them say, that when he first came into the neighbourhood, he was the most gloomy and unsociable being in the world, supposed to be breaking his heart for the loss of his wife. Poor man! he seems very lonely even now, but perhaps it may end in Katherine's consoling him. Certainly she is pleased when he comes, and that has been tolerably often of late. I have fancied, sometimes, that one of his great attractions, in her eyes, is the fact of his not caring for music. You see, most of the people here think a good deal of my singing, and although I am known to be only *what I am*, whenever I join in the concerts, or even sing alone, for the amusement of those who are staying in the house, I get a considerable degree of attention for the time; and Katherine, who will never touch either harp or piano now, sinks temporarily into the shade. This, I can well believe, is both galling and humiliating to her, and therefore it is but natural that she should feel kindly disposed towards Mr. Mervyn, who acknowledges openly that he does not care for music, and is incapable of giving an opinion concerning the finest voice that man or woman ever possessed. This is peculiar, is it not?— but then he is highly intellectual—the only *very* intellectual man I have ever in all my life come in contact with; and yet you remember what a marvel of lofty intelligence my ideal hero used to be.

" Well, well, those old foolish dreamings had a strange sweetness in them, and I cannot feel sorry for that which made my youth so bright, though truly the reality has been nothing, no-thing like it. Don't let me, however, run away from Mr. Mervyn again just yet, because I have more to tell you about him.

"I was taking one of my favourite walks a fortnight ago, nurse and baby accompanying me as usual, when who should I suddenly stumble on, in a little sheltered glen, that I fancied nobody but myself ever visited, but this very gentleman, sitting under a tree (though it was a cold, windy day,) with a book in his hand. Of course, I was going to bow and pass on. To tell you the truth, it was one of my bad days, and I had been crying till I was certain my eyes were quite red and swollen, and by no means fit to be seen!

"Mr. Mervyn, however, rose immediately, and after he had shaken hands, continued to walk beside me as simply and naturally as if such an action could by no possibility be objected to, or misconstrued. I think, when people's minds are filled with a great sorrow or regret, they forget the foolish conventionalities of the world, and suffer themselves to be guided by the far pleasanter laws of kindness and natural impulse.

" I am sure this was the case with him, for turning round abruptly to look into my face, he saw that I had been crying, and asked me, in quite a brotherly way, what was the matter. I said it was nothing particular—only I felt so desolate. I had felt so ever since my husband went away.

" 'And that is bad enough, God knows !' he replied, in a low, thoughtful voice. 'I have felt it; I know what it is to be desolate, and in a manner that I trust *you* will never understand.'

" I believe I shuddered, for he continued, with increased gravity.

" 'It is nothing, comparatively nothing, so

long as those we love are in the same world with us—we can hope, and look forward, in the worst of cases, and interchange thoughts, and go on loving as fondly and truly as if we were side by side—but when Death comes and places his barrier of ice between us, forbidding us even to love what the worms have claimed—ah, this is very, very different.'

"It was he who shuddered now, and I, feeling just ready to sob aloud, made some commonplace, incoherent remark about death being indeed a terrible thing, and his case far worse than mine.

"'And I have no child, no little one to comfort *me*,' he said, appearing determined to excite my pity to the utmost.

"Here a sudden and remarkable impulse prompted me to reply—'I hope, however, you have *that Friend*, who has promised to supply

to those who seek Him, the loss of all besides.'

"'If I understand you rightly, I have not,' he
said, in a colder, harder voice. 'I am not a
religious man, even in the broadest signification
of the term, and certainly still less so, in the
way I suppose you mean. Do you often choose
these solitary places for your rambles, Mrs.
Willand?'

"I saw, of course, that he meant to change
the subject; and, therefore, during the re-
mainder of our walk (for he would go as far as
the house with me) we spoke on indifferent
matters, and he greatly interested me by his
originality and varied information. I do sincerely hope that Mr. Mervyn will marry Katherine, for I believe if she were happy, she
would be more amiable, and if he loved her, she
could not fail of being happy with him.

"Since I have been here, I have had two or three letters from Mr. Arnold (my 'guardian,' as Sydney would always persist in calling him), and he writes so seriously, so earnestly on religious subjects, that I have been led to think a great deal of late concerning *the One thing needful.* It *is this*, you know, dear Norah, notwithstanding all our obstinate indifference, and trying to put off the solemn consideration of it as long as we possibly can. Oh that I had fewer wasted years, fewer neglected opportunities, fewer unappreciated privileges to look back upon and deplore !

"But now I know you are beginning to yawn, so I will inflict no more of my gloominess upon you. When I have anything interesting to tell you, I will write again. Good bye, dear Norah.

"Yours ever affectionately,

"NELLY."

CHAPTER V.

As the winter advanced—the cold, bleak, sunless winter, whose influence only the gayest and happiest can entirely withstand, Ellen's "bad days" became of more frequent occurrence, and her seasons of hope and cheerfulness very few and far between.

Her husband's letters, though always eagerly welcomed, were but poor substitutes for his presence—that presence which had surrounded her with an atmosphere of love and tenderness, scarcely acknowledged indeed while it was with her, but bitterly, bitterly missed and wept for, after it was gone.

She was feeling ill, too, as she invariably did in the winter, and yearning ever more and more passionately for that actual, personal heart sympathy, which none here were likely to bestow upon her.

Mr. Wilmot, it is true, had been from the first most kind and considerate; and had championship been needed, there is no doubt that he would have stood forth as Ellen's warmest champion; but seeing that his womenkind were disposed to treat her civilly, and that amongst his guests she was rather a favourite than otherwise, this somewhat dreamy old gentleman, who liked his own snug little library far better than the large, crowded drawing-rooms, soon forgot that Ellen did not belong of right to the family, and ceased to notice her in any particular way.

Mrs. Wilmot, being full of anxiety about Katherine, and having so many visitors to entertain, had literally no time, even if she had had the inclination, to remark whether Sydney's wife were well or ill, dull or gay; and Katherine herself, though doubtless she saw more than the others, made no open observations on Ellen's changes of looks or moods, thinking, it may be, that the happiness she *had* enjoyed, ought to be sufficient to last a life-time.

But to the little May (who had grown into a fine, healthy child) cousin Katherine was all affection and tenderness. She liked to have it with her in her own private room, crawling on the warm, rich carpet, or trying to steady itself against the low, soft ottomans and couches, that seemed gathered here for the tiny lady's especial benefit. And devoted as Ellen was to her child, and fearful of having it for long out of her sight, she knew—knew for a certainty now, that the proud, imperious Katherine would take as much care of May as if the baby were her own.

Once, when the greater and the lesser cousin were spending their morning together in the fashion above described, and Ellen was practising a new song in the drawing-room, Mr. Mervyn was suddenly announced.

There happened at this time to be no visitors staying in the house.

"I will go and send Mrs. Wilmot and Katherine to you," said Ellen, after she had risen and shaken hands with the gentleman, who was speedily seated, as if for a long visit, by the blazing fire.

"No, don't," he replied, in his simple, un-conventional manner. "I would much rather talk to you for a little while. Your fingers must be very cold. Why cannot you sit down and warm them ?"

Ellen blushed slightly (for she had not got over that foolish habit even yet), but accepted the invitation, thinking that perhaps he had something to say concerning Katherine, who was evidently getting to like him very well indeed.

" I wanted to ask you," he began, " whether you had heard from your husband lately; and also if you are still feeling as desolate and un-happy as you were some time ago."

" This is very kind of you," Ellen replied ; and being all unused now-a-days to the expression of any particular interest in herself or her feelings, from those around her, she really considered it remarkably so, and was touched by it.

"Not in the least kind," he said again.

"You are the first person I have met since I came to Scotland, who has appeared to me to be suffering as I have suffered myself; and it is not only natural but inevitable, that I should feel a little sympathy for you, will you answer my questions?"

"Thank you. I had forgotten, I heard from my husband about ten days ago ; he writes by every mail. As for my desolation and loneliness, that can't be helped, you know. I must endure it."

"They are kind to you here—are they not?"

"Oh yes, I have nothing to complain of."

"And yet you are very unhappy ; I can see that. I daresay your husband petted you a great deal, was the lover as well as the husband ; and with a disposition like yours, you would miss all this cruelly. I understand it perfectly."

Did he ? Then he ought not to have talked about it, unless he meant to derive gratification from the sight of Ellen's emotion.

She really could not help shedding a few tears, when he alluded to that love which every day and every hour she felt the want of, and was so unfitted to dispense with, even for a time.

Mr. Mervyn made no comment, however, on her tears—perhaps he thought they would do her good. And presently he spoke again.

" If you care for reading, and have exhausted the light literature of the Glens, I can always supply you with books. I get the newest and best from England once a month."

" Thank you, I shall be very glad. They do not read much here."

" Not even Miss Katherine ?"

" No, but then she has not been well for a

long time—And that reminds me, that I had better call her now. Mrs. Wilmot would think it strange if I did not."

" As you like ; but I must be going almost immediately. Shall I send you a packet of books this evening ?"

" If it will not be troubling you too much."

" I shall be happy in affording you the small-est pleasure."

Ellen was leaving the room, not intending to return to it again till he was gone.

" Good-bye, Mrs. Willand. Why won't you say good-bye ?"

She returned, with a slight smile, and shook hands with him.

Then finding Katherine, and telling her who was down stairs, Ellen devoted the rest of the morning to her little daughter.

It was nearly a month after this, when she

again wrote to Norah. The following is an extract from her letter.

" I am afraid things are not progressing very rapidly between Katherine and Mr. Mervyn, and lately she has not seemed to care so much whether he comes or stays away. Perhaps he has disgusted her, by being kind to me; for he is very, very kind, and I am not ashamed of showing that I am grateful. You would not wonder if you knew how my very soul had been crying out for kindness and sympathy, like that poor blind girl I read of, in a book he lent me.

' A branch of ivy, dying in the ground.'

" I need some bough to twine around, but don't be alarmed for me, dear Norah; I love my poor Sydney far, far too well to be in danger of feeling more than gratitude towards any one, however good they may be to me.

"Katherine knows he lends me books—indeed, I never meant to make a secret of it; why should I ? and she says I ought to feel highly flattered, by the notice of so clever and intellectual a man as Mr. Mervyn. She does not show in the least that she is annoyed by it. She *may* think that it is done out of compliment to herself—but no, Katherine is a proud, but not a vain woman. I don't believe she has any idea that Mr. Mervyn is in love with her. Nor is he, of this I am very sure, and indeed I doubt whether there is a woman in ten thousand who would really suit him, even if he wished to marry again, which probally he does not. You see I talk a good deal with him now, whenever he is here, and I begin to know a little, still only a little of his character. You, Norah, would

admire him, even more than I do, he is so very,
very clever; and what I think people who
understand these things better than I do, would
call metaphysical. He likes to talk on subjects
that are utterly beyond my comprehension, and
to get into regions where I cannot possibly follow him, and then, poor man! he looks so disappointed—sometimes even a little cross, I fancy,
and goes away abruptly—as if I could help not
being as intellectual as he is. Still, for all this,
his great kindness has been an immense boon
to me. It has given an interest to the dull,
cheerless life I was leading, and enabled me to
get through the winter far better than I had
dared to hope.

"Did I tell you that Maurice and Gracie are
to be married early in April, and that mamma
is going back to our own cottage as soon as
they are settled at St. Ives? God bless them

all, all my dear absent ones, and make them as happy as they deserve to be.

. " My mother-in-law is again in Paris, her earthly Eden, it seems. She was to have spent the winter here, but thought better of it. By the bye, I should have been badly off, had Sydney taken her at her word, about supplying me with pocket-money in his absence; but he must have guessed what her promises were worth, for he has already twice forwarded to me a large sum out of his salary, and I feel myself quite a rich woman, having little occasion for spending money here.

" I am so glad, Norah, that you have at length been persuaded (I can fancy with what difficulty) to publish some of your poems. You will be famous in the world of letters yet, and I shall be duly proud of having such a celebrity for my friend. I wish I could bring you and

Mr. Mervyn together, for I am certain——
Well, never mind; stranger things have happened, and who can tell? A message to say
he is below, and wants to see me. I will
finish my letter after the interview."

*   *   *   *   *

" Alas! it was to say good-bye. He is
going to England immediately, on business of
importance, connected with his succession to
the estates which he owns in this country, and
to inherit which, I believe, I have heard that he
had to change his name. Now there is some
technical dispute about it, he tells me, and he
may be kept for months about those tiresome
law courts, and all for the merest trifle. He
was evidently terribly put out, and reluctant to
go.

" I said I was very sorry, (as indeed I am) and he replied bluntly, that he hoped I was; for that he needed some little consolation to render such a journey, at this time of the year, endurable.

"I don't exactly see how my being sorry can be a consolation to him, unless indeed (which I have never suspected) he has as strong a craving for sympathy and affection as myself, and has found pleasure, as well as given it, in his kindness to me.

" I shall be so happy in introducing him to Sydney at some future time, although they are so very, very different—oh, how different! Yet I think they will like each other for my sake—a bit of the old vanity creeping out, you will say, but I don't believe it *is* vanity in this case. Mr. Mervyn *does* like me, in spite of his vast superiority; and as for my dear husband, ah, you know all about that.

"In bidding me good-bye, Mr. Mervyn said he hoped I understood that his whole library was at my service—that he had left orders with his housekeeper to admit either myself, or anybody I chose to send for books, at all times; and that he should feel really hurt if I abstained from doing as he wished. Of course I thanked him again and again. Could I help being grateful?—and then we parted like old friends who truly esteem each other.

"And now my only bit of interest and comfort connected with the Glens is gone, perhaps, for ever, and I feel to-night, Norah, so sad and weary, that if it were not for May—bless her!—and my poor, poor Sydney, far away, I could be glad to close my tired eyes, and never open them again on this strange, strange world. Write to me soon, and

"Believe me always

"Your faithful and loving

"NELLY."

CHAPTER VI.

A MAIL had come in and brought no letter from Sydney.

It was the very first time such a thing had happened, and Ellen could not help feeling a good deal of anxiety about it.

Mr. Wilmot did his best to reassure her— bade her remember the countless trifling accidents that might have occurred to prevent her husband's letter being posted in time, the negligence of a servant, some unexpected business at the last moment, even some change in the hour of closing the mail-bags, which Sydney might have been unaware of—any of these things would have produced the same result, and were quite likely to have happened.

How often persons who had friends at a distance worried themselves nearly to death from the non-arrival of letters, and then discovered, after all, that their anxiety had been utterly causeless.

All this was very true; and having it patiently repeated to her day by day, (for the kind old gentleman could not bear to see the young wife looking so pale and restless,) Ellen at length took comfort, and believed that she had been frightened at a shadow.

The worst of the winter was over now, and she was able occasionally to renew the walks that in the autumn had given her so much pleasure. The wild bleakness of the scenery suited her present state of mind ; and once out upon the lonely hills, with the rough north wind making its weird-like music around her, Ellen felt little inclination to return to the house, which was again filled with gay visitors, and where she never seemed to have any definite or lawful place.

One morning as she was crossing the hall with her bonnet and cloak on, in preparation for a long solitary ramble, (the day being too . cold for May to accompany her,) Katherine suddenly opened the door of a room she often occupied, and asked Ellen if she would like a companion.

"Who is it?" was the quick reply, for in truth the proposal was anything but agreeable.

" Myself."

" *You*, Katherine ? Why, you never walk,

and you know I generally go immense dis-
tances."

"Well, I daresay I could do as much, if I
tried. At any rate, if you have no particular
objection, I will put my things on. They are
all going to drive with mamma, to see some
lion of the neighbourhood this morning; and I
hate sight-seeing."

"Come with me, then," said Ellen; for how
could she say anything else?

Mental query.—What was Katherine's object in this apparently unaccountable freak?

A very plausible one, if not the true one,
soon became manifest.

"Ellen," she said, after they had been walking side by side for about ten minutes without
speaking, " have you ever seen Mr. Mervyn's
house? It is situated, I believe, in one of the
valleys on the other side of those hills to the

left.   Mamma tells me it is a beautiful place.   I had my reasons for not going there before, but I think now he is away it would be a good opportunity.   Can we get so far?"

" We might, I suppose, for I have been all over the hills, though never far down on the other side; but I am afraid you would be very tired."

" Oh no, it will do me good.   I want to be tired, for I seldom sleep at night,—sleep well, I mean—besides, we can rest there. I know the housekeeper has orders to receive any of us if we happen to go; and you have never yet availed yourself of Mr. Mervyn's offer about the books."

" No, I have not had much inclination for reading lately."

" Are you still anxious about letters?"

"Not so anxious as I was ; but still it fidgets me at times."

"You should not let it. I daresay what my father suggests is true."

Second mental query.—What had come over Katherine that she should speak in this way?

"God grant it may be !" Ellen said : "poor dear Sydney, if he were ill, and I not there—"

"Most unlikely," replied Katherine with a return of her old sharpness—"I never knew Sydney ill, or heard of his being ill, since he was born."

"He had indeed excellent health, though to look at him you would scarcely think so."

After a pause, Katherine said with assumed carelessness, and as if she were continuing the subject rather out of compliment to the wife, than from any personal interest in the matter—

"Was not Sydney an extremely disorderly,

unpunctual man? just the person who would be likely to put off writing till the last moment, or forget to send a letter till it was too late?"

"Not a letter to me," said Ellen quickly; but a thought flashing across her mind, she added immediately—"it is true, however, that he was always very irregular and uncertain; and as Mr. Wilmot says, there are so many things that might have happened."

"So many things," repeated Katherine musingly; and then they walked on very fast, and in total silence, for at least half-an hour.

- The distance to Mr. Mervyn's house was much greater than they had either of them reckoned on; and meeting so few persons of whom they could make enquiries, it was with considerable difficulty that they found the house at all.

Katherine was completely knocked up, as she was obliged to acknowledge; and when the housekeeper, on their sending in their cards, hastened out and begged the ladies to walk into the library, where she always had a little fire, Miss Wilmot threw herself on the nearest chair, and gave every indication of an approaching fainting fit.

But with the aid of cold water, and some strong essence, which was fortunately at hand, this catastrophe was for the time averted, and after about ten minutes' rest, she declared herself quite recovered.

The housekeeper then fetched some wine and cake, entreated the ladies to make themselves comfortable, and said she would go and gather a bouquet from the hothouses, as " master" had desired her to do, should either of the young ladies from the Glens ever come to Heath Vale while he was away.

" A most finished gentleman, this friend of

yours !" said Katherine, when Ellen and herself were left together—" don't you think so ?"

" I think he is very kind—no doubt his suffering has taught him to be so."

" Why should it ? For my part I know nothing that sours the temper so much as suffering. It is very easy for people who are happy to be amiable."

" I think, with you, that the *immediate* effect of suffering is anything but improving to the character; but when it is over, and we have only got to look back upon it as a thing gone · for ever, then I know it often has a most softening and blessed influence."

" But some kinds of suffering are never over, at least in this life; how then ?"

" Ah, I cannot say what would be the result in such a case, though we do hear of people going through one continued martyrdom, either physical or mental, and being cheerful and contented (consequently not unamiable) to the end."

"Yes, but those are your saints and heroines. I am speaking only of poor ordinary mortals, who have nothing but their own strength or pride to sustain them. Poor wretches! how are they to grow amiable when every faculty is engaged in hiding their wounds from the prying eyes around them?"

"But," said Ellen, more and more surprised that Katherine should enter with her on such subjects—"there is no moral necessity for suffering being concealed at all. Few are so desolate that they cannot find at least one friendly heart that will listen to, and sympathize with their trouble."

"Which brings us back to our starting point," said Katherine, resuming her ordinary manner—"for Mr. Mervyn has, I am sure, been very sympathizing towards you. How do you like his house?"

"It seems a charming place, and everything in such beautiful order. Do you know, Katherine, I used to hope when we were first acquainted with Mr. Mervyn, that you would one day be the mistress of it."

"Very kind of you indeed. And what made you cease to hope it?"

"I ceased to *expect* it, when I saw how indifferent you were to the gentleman himself."

"And also how indifferent the gentleman was to me—be truthful, Ellen. I can bear it."

"Well, yes; but had you been warmer in your manner to him, it might have been otherwise."

"Never. He would want to be adored, and looked up to, and my vocation does not lie in that direction. Perhaps he will bring a wife back with him."

"It is possible he may."

"But I don't expect it, neither do you. Come, take some wine and cake, and then we must be thinking of getting back.   I wish I had thought of ordering the pony carriage to come for us."

"I fear you will never walk it, without making yourself quite ill."

"By the bye, Mr. Mervyn has carriage and horses doing nothing. Let us ring the bell, and ask if we cannot be driven home?"

"Would it not be taking a liberty? You know he is very peculiar in some things."

"Nonsense!—it will be doing him a great honour.   Ring at once."

Ellen obeyed; and on the appearance of the housekeeper, Katherine made the request.

"To be sure you can, ma'am," was the prompt

reply, presenting, as she spoke, a magnificent bouquet of flowers to Miss Wilmot. "I should have taken the liberty of proposing it in any case, for it is a great distance from where you live, and master will be so sorry when he hears that you were taken ill. But, before you go, ma'am, please to walk in here—(opening a small door at one end of the room)—this is where master keeps his favourite books, and he told me if you came, to be sure and show you in here, and beg you to choose whatever you thought proper."

Katherine looked at Ellen, and smiled. It' was evident that she had been taken for the lady on whose behalf all these instructions had been given; and it was not worth while to rectify the mistake.

Nothing could be more natural, Ellen herself decided, as in passing into the inner room she caught a view of her own and Katherine's face in a large, antique mirror. Till this moment, she had never thought of noticing how strangely her youthful beauty had faded, how little remained of that Hebe brightness and freshness, for which, before her marriage, she had been so remarkable. The golden hair no longer flowing in natural ringlets, but plainly braided over the forehead, (for what object had she in taking pains with it now?) gave quite a new expression to the countenance; and the eyes that had shed so many tears, had lost that sparkling, sunny look, without which blue eyes can rarely be called beautiful. A few persons, it is true, might have preferred Ellen as she now was; but then it would have been on a second examination of the face, which had retained none of its striking characteristics. Beholding it now, in contrast with Katherine's, Ellen thought it both plain and unpleasing; and glancing down at her simple morning dress, a dark, warm tartan with cloak to match—she was not surprised that Mr. Mervyn's housekeeper should instinctively select the tall, elegantly attired, and really hand- some Katherine as the lady most likely to be the object of her master's attentions, and concerning whom he had left' so many polite orders.

" Will you take any books ?" Katherine asked, as they found themselves again alone in a snugly- furnished and thoroughly bachelor-looking little sanctum ; "you have choice enough, however difficult you may be."

" I don't know,—for see what hard, dry, philosophical books the greater part of them are. Here is one shelf devoted to light litera- ture. I will take a volume of Scott's poetry. Mr. Mervyn is rather an admirer of it. I sup- pose all Scotchmen are."

"But he is not a Scotchman—surely you knew that ?"

"On the contrary, I fancied he had a very decided accent."

"An Irish accent, if you like. At all events he is an Irishman."

"Is it possible?—well, I am astonished."

"That he should have concealed the fact from you?"

"No—it is nothing to me, only it would have been so natural for him to mention it."

"I believe some of his near relatives are Scotch—certainly the cousin was, who left him his present name and this estate ;—but here comes the old woman again, so I suppose the carriage is ready. Let us go at once. I have had enough of this."

Katherine had laid down her bouquet on the library table, and was going away without remembering it. The housekeeper ran after her, and proffered it once more, with some remark to the effect that Mr. Mervyn would be vexed if he heard she had not accepted his flowers.

" Give them to the other lady," Miss Wilmot replied then, with one of her most majestic looks, —" that is Mrs. Willand."

The poor woman, half-frightened and half-abashed, turned to the now blushing Ellen.

"I beg your pardon, ma'am,—will you be pleased to have the flowers?—but master said I was to gather them for either of the ladies from the Glens."

"Thank you. They are very beautiful, and I am delighted to have them," she replied with her usual graciousness, which certainly gave her, for the time, an attraction Katherine never possessed. "We are much obliged, both to you and to Mr. Mervyn, for this kind reception."

The housekeeper made a low curtsey, handed the two ladies into the carriage, and told the coachman where he was to take them.

"A most courtly old dame," observed Katherine, as they drove off, "and quite appropriate to the house and its master.—Oh, how tired I am!"

"But you should have kept the flowers," Ellen said, in a vexed tone, "you know you had as much right to them as myself. If I could believe otherwise, do you suppose I would have taken them, beautiful as they are? What will Mr. Mervyn think, if the woman repeats what you have said to him?"

"What do I care?—Anything is better than his thinking I want his attentions. Of course, it does not signify about *you*, as a married woman; but if I had not set that stupid old thing right, and she had told him that I took the flowers, he would have imagined that I was only waiting for him to make love to me."

Ellen thought the explanation a lame one, but it was useless pursuing the subject; and she could only determine to keep more out of Mr. Mervyn's way for the future, lest Katherine, in one of her wicked moods, should make use of the kindly feeling existing between them, as a weapon against her.

Oh how fervently she wished her husband would return to shield her from the very possibility of such things. How her heart yearned towards him also, as she reflected on her waning beauty, and felt sure, quite sure that his was a love that would stand far severer tests than even this. She had never done him justice, never been half kind and affectionate enough to him when they had been together— but oh it should be so different when he came home again ; he should see that she too could love, that she too could be unselfish ; and, above all, that she could appreciate that true and perfect devotion, which he had always manifested towards her, and would manifest—she was certain of it—to the end.

"Oh, how tired I am," said Katherine once more, as having been safely deposited at the entrance to their own grounds, she accepted the offer of Ellen's arm to walk up to the house.

"You look very tired. I should recommend you to lie down and keep quiet till dinner time."

"If I can—but there are *some* moods in which to keep quiet is simply a thing impossible, however weary the body may be. What are *you* going to do?"

"To see May first of all ; and then, perhaps, to write a letter or two."

" Well then, if I come to your room in about half an hour, perhaps you will spare the child to me."

" Certainly."

On reaching her room, Ellen found two letters waiting for her—one from Norah and the other from Mrs. Lane, with whom (since their meeting at Brompton) she had kept up a pretty regular correspondence.

But May had the first claim upon the mother's time and attention—she had been wanting mamma all the morning—so the letters were put aside to be read when aunt Katherine came to fetch her playfellow; and Ellen, unmindful of her own fatigue, devoted herself for the stipulated half hour to her darling's amusement, and yielded her up reluctantly at last.

This talking to and romping with the

merry little child, was such a pleasant way of getting" rid of all anxious and disagreeable thoughts.

But now came her letters, and they too gave her something, besides the matters that had been recently pressing on her mind, to reflect about. Mrs. Lane's certainly contained no· thing new, but then her earnest and deeply serious mode of writing, like that of Mr. Arnold's, (only, if possible, more earnest, more serious) always, for the time at least, directed Ellen's thoughts into an unworldly channel, and forced upon her a self-examination which was sure to be rather humiliating than agreeable.

But Norah's letter, in addition to its usual amount of pleasant, clever chit-chat, contained something which struck Ellen very much indeed. It was this—

"I must tell you, Nelly, that you have not

succeeded in making me like your Mr. Mervyn.
I do not even trust him; and I say it boldly,
in defiance of the indignation which I am
nearly sure so uncharitable an opinion will
elicit. Perhaps I may be wrong—but old
maid as I am getting on to be, (yes, indeed—I
am nearer thirty than twenty) I have seen a
little of the world, and I have not one atom of
faith in platonic friendship. Neither do I like
your sentimental quotation about the ivy. It
is all nonsense; and yet, you know, I have my
share of romance and sentiment too—only I
shall take good care that it never leads me into
mischief. Take you care also, Mrs. Nelly—
and endure the feelings of loneliness and desolation you complain of, patiently—until your
good, kind husband comes home to comfort you.

"And now having proved my right to the
title of friend by making myself thus disagree-

able, I embrace you affectionately, and sub-
scribe myself

"Your sincere and devoted

"NORAH."

It made Ellen very grave, if not uncomfortable, and it took her thoughts back to long,
long ago, before her marriage, when she had
once spoken (she could not in the least remember how it came about) on the subject of platonic friendship with John Arnold. He did
not believe in it either—Ellen remembered
that perfectly. And yet how very, very sure
she felt of herself with regard to Mr. Mervyn!
And of him too.

She wished she had said nothing about him
to Norah. It was so exceedingly ridiculous,
and not pleasant either, to be warned in that
authoritative manner, when there was not the

shadow of danger near. And then too it was doing a great injustice to Mr. Mervyn! the unsuspecting kind-hearted, melancholy man, who lived more in the past than in the present, and whose only passion was the study of things that even Norah herself would find it difficult to understand.

But, at any rate, these hints, as well as the occurrences of the morning, would serve for a useful lesson. Ellen knew there was a command to cease from all *appearance* of evil, and it did not cost her much to resolve upon a line of conduct that should widen the distance between herself and Mr. Mervyn. She would be sorry for him to think her ungrateful, but even this was better—anything was better than giving occasion for one breath of slander or suspicion.

The very thought of such a thing brought

burning blushes to her cheek, and she had not
yet recovered her composure, when Katherine,
dressed for dinner, came in with May, and told
Ellen she had no time to lose, if she intended
making any change in her toilette.

What could possess this girl to obtrude her
society so often to-day upon one she rarely spoke
to, or even looked at, when they were unavoid-
ably in the same room?

As they were going down together, she said,
in quite a careless way, as if she had just remembered it—

"I suppose papa has not mentioned to you
that there is a possibility of getting letters from
South America to-day or to-morrow? An extra
mail that was sent out with some dispatches for
Government arrived in London on the twelfth,
and this, you know, is the fifteenth."

Ellen's heart was beating so rapidly that she

could not immediately reply. They passed, at that moment, under the great lamp in the hall.

"Good gracious, Ellen, how white you are! I thought you would be so pleased."

"If there *are* letters—but if not—"

"Don't be ridiculous and fanciful. Of course there will be."

Ellen turned round instinctively to look at the speaker. She wanted to get encouragement by any means—a sickness like death had suddenly come over her. Perhaps Katherine knew something!

She might well think so; when she saw the face of her companion, it was whiter and more full of restless excitement than her own.

"Katherine, Katherine! what is it—what do you know? For God's sake don't keep me in this terrible suspense."

She had laid hold of a chair for support, but the disengaged hand was grasping Katherine tightly, imploringly. She could not get away.

"Ellen, I give you my word, my solemn word, I know nothing—let me go."

"Then why are you so pale and agitated? Why have you been haunting me all day?"

"Very flattering, certainly," and Katherine tried to laugh, "but I have told you the simple truth. I knew only this morning that letters could arrive. I am sorry I said a word about it, for I fear, for to-night at least, it is too late."

"Katherine, you are anxious yourself, *and it is for the same cause.*"

She spoke under great excitement, though not angrily—it was not anger that she felt. Katherine looked at her steadily for a moment; she would have kept up her pride and dignity at any cost, at the cost even of a lie, if she could ; but nature, previously half-exhausted, lent her no assistance now ; and with one brief shudder, Katherine sank upon the chair that Ellen had been holding, and fainted.

CHAPTER VII.

FOR the next half-hour all was confusion and excitement in the great house, where a real fainting fit was a thing hitherto unknown.

Mrs. Wilmot was too much frightened and bewildered to be of any use to her daughter. She could only ask rapid questions of everybody as to the cause of this sudden illness, and rail at Ellen, (who did not take in a word she said, on account of her own excitement), when she heard of the walk to Mr. Mervyn's in the morning.

Fortunately, some of the female guests knew what remedies to apply, and the young lady was, therefore, soon restored to consciousness, and laid upon a sofa in the drawing-room, Ellen remaining, as well as her own maid, to watch beside her, while the rest of the party went in to dinner.

"What a fuss!" said Katherine, as soon as she found strength to speak, "as if nobody had ever fainted in all the world till now—where is papa?"

Ellen had been wondering what had become of Mr. Wilmot, and longing for the moment when she might see him alone, and ask him about this mail from Guatemala.

"I don't know," she replied, "he has not been into the drawing-room since you were brought here; he cannot have heard of your illness."

" But they will tell him now, surely. I wish
he would come and speak to me."

" Shall I go to the dining-room and ask
him ?"

" No, let Justine go."

The girl was sent.

" You see, Ellen, you were right when you
said that walk would be too much for me. This
had been threatening me all day, and you made
me nervous by looking so pale and frightened.
You are not anxious now, are you ?"

" Yes."

" Well, papa will reassure you ; of course it
is all right, it would make even me, who am
only his cousin, miserable, were I to think
otherwise. Why doesn't papa come ?"

Ellen said nothing, but sat with her straining
eyes fixed upon the door, through which Mr.
Wilmot would have to enter from the dining-

room. She had that strong foreboding of evil weighing upon her mind, which forbids the expression of ordinary anxiety, which can only wrap itself in its own chill mantle, and wait!

Wait for a confirmation of those fears which are sure not to be behind the reality, and are very, very often, happily in advance of it.

At length Justine returned.

" Your papa has not come in to dinner, Miss. He sent word that he had received letters of importance, and should be engaged for another hour in the library. They have just taken some soup to him there, and your mamma, Miss, hopes you are better, and will soon come to you."

Ellen had risen before this speech of Justine's was half finished, but seeing how deadly pale Katherine had become again, she waited till its conclusion, and then said, in a voice that betrayed how fast her heart was beating,

"I will go to the library at once. I cannot bear this suspense. There *must* be something."

"And I will come too!" (in great excitement, and attempting to rise as she spoke.)

"No, no, Katherine, you are not fit to move, you would faint directly, besides," (forcing her to lie down again), " if there is anything bad to hear, I, I only, have the right to hear it, and I must hear it *alone*. I am his wife, Katherine."

It may be doubted whether she knew at all what she was saying, so agonizing had her fears become, but the earnestness of her manner had the effect of keeping Katherine quiet, and she submitted to be left with her maid.

It surely could not have been accident that brought so vividly to Ellen's remembrance (as she traversed the short space between the drawing-room and Mr. Wilmot's library) those words, spoken to her by Mrs. Lane, on the last occasion of their being together. "I believe that you will have a rough and thorny path to tread, for whom the Lord loveth He chasteneth, and has He not already given some proofs of loving you?" It could not, I repeat, have been merely accident, because it imparted to her a strength that seemed, even to herself, unnatural.

And so she reached the library-door, knocked gently, and then went in.

Mr. Wilmot was sitting at the centre table with his face buried in his hands; he had not heard the knock, nor the softly-opening door.

By the light of a faint lamp, Ellen saw a

large, unfolded letter on the table beside him.
The writing was bold and straggling, very
different to Sydney's delicate, almost feminine
characters.

Perhaps it had nothing to do with Sydney
at all.

Nerved by this hope, Ellen advanced into
the room—went close to Mr. Wilmot—
touched him on the shoulder.

He started violently, looked up, saw who
it was, and recoiled as if from some painful
vision.

"I beg your pardon—"

"No, no," he said, hastily interrupting her,
"you have done nothing wrong. Poor child,
poor child!"

Then the old man took her into his arms,
crying himself like a woman, and held her
there, while her wild, passionate sobs shook

them both, and made him fear very seriously that he had killed her by his abruptness.

And yet he had said nothing, absolutely nothing, beyond those words, " poor child, poor child !"

But in addition to this, Ellen's wandering eyes had lighted upon one single, brief sentence in the open letter, and so she knew that the love which a few short hours ago she had been dwelling on with such grateful remembrance, such fond delight, was gone from her *for ever !*

She knew that her husband *was dead !*—that she was a widow, and her little child fatherless.

That they were both destitute in the world.

She thought of it all, even in those first moments of unspeakable misery, for it is a mistake to suppose that a violent shock like this *necessarily* destroys for the time the thinking and reasoning powers. With some minds it may certainly do so, it appears most natural that it should; but with others, I know that the effect produced is exactly the reverse of this, and that they see the whole future consequences of a sudden misfortune at the very moment it is communicated to them.

Mr. Wilmot was greatly to be pitied in the circumstances under which he found himself. He knew he ought to say something consoling, something soothing at the least, to the poor, desolate young creature, sobbing, as it seemed, her very life away, in his arms; but he was so excessively grieved himself, he had been so particularly fond of Sydney, that all he could think of, in connection with the sad event, would have proved the reverse of comfort-

ing, and so he said nothing, but suffered her
to cry on.

This was, after all, the best course he could
have pursued with her, for when nature became
quite exhausted, the extreme mental torture
ceased; and although Ellen was not fortunate
enough to faint, as Katherine, under far less
trying circumstances, had done, a certain
numbness of the faculties succeeded the wild
excitement of her first anguish; and in this
state Mr. Wilmot laid her down, and then, sum-
moning assistance, got her safely carried to bed.

She was so very passive and quiet now, that
it did not occur to them there would be any necessity for calling in medical advice; and indeed,
when the cause of all this came to be known,
there was so much excitement prevailing in the
household, so much " talking over " the sudden
and melancholy event which had made poor Mrs.

Sydney a widow, that Mrs. Sydney herself was in danger of being neglected, and certainly would have been, but for Mr. Wilmot and her little girl's nurse, who, having lived with Ellen since her marriage, was really attached to her on her own account.

These two remained with her some time after she had been laid upon her bed ; but they were both deceived by her perfect quietness, and thought that the worst was over. Mr. Wilmot suggested a composing draught to be taken the last thing, and that nurse should make up a bed for herself, on the ground, near her mistress.

Then bending to look closely into the fixed, tearless eyes, that seemed all unconscious of his scrutiny, a film gathered over his own, and he told the woman to watch carefully and to call him, if he could be of the least service.

He found his wife crying in the drawing-room, and surrounded by half-a-dozen of her female guests, all talking very fast, and persuading themselves that they were of immense comfort to the poor, dear woman, who had lost her nephew so suddenly.

"Where is Kate?" he asked abruptly, thinking that she, at least, might have gone to Ellen.

"Oh, in bed I hope by this time," replied Mrs. Wilmot, beginning to sob afresh at the sight of her husband. "You did not hear that she fainted before dinner, from having over-walked herself this morning."

"Fainted?—No, I did not know that she was given to that sort of thing. Poor Kate! has she heard?"

"Yes. Unfortunately, Justine, the instant she got hold of the news, ran into the room where Katherine was lying after her fainting fit, and told everything. I have not seen her since, because she went up-stairs at once, and sent me word that she did not wish to be disturbed again for the night; she was going to bed."

"Is Justine with her?"

"Yes—and the door locked. I am sure she will let nobody in."

"Well, I wish before you go to bed yourself, you would look in upon poor Ellen. There is something about her eyes that I don't quite like."

"They told me she was perfectly composed, now."

"So she is, apparently—but go and judge for yourself. It has been a fearful blow for her."

Mrs. Wilmot was really not a hard-hearted woman, and the sight of Ellen's corpse-like face, not only as regarded its pallor, but in respect to the fixed rigidity of the features, affected her very much indeed; and she inquired eagerly of the nurse whether there was nothing to be done.

"I believe not yet, ma'am," replied the woman, who had been watching her charge attentively since Mr. Wilmot's departure. "Even if we could make her cry, she is too exhausted to bear it. Sleep will be her best chance; and this we must force by laudanum."

"You are sure it will be right?"

"Quite sure, ma'am—for if she doesn't sleep, she will be dead, or next thing to it, by morning."

"Had we not better send for a doctor?"

"He could do no good here at present— nature will have its way."

Then the mother thought of her own daughter, and wondered anxiously what effect the news of Sydney's death would have upon her.

Happily for her maternal sensibilities, she had not the faintest notion of what was really going on in Katherine's room. Had it been otherwise, she could not so composedly have bidden her numerous guests good-night, or expressed so politely her regrets that this sudden family affliction should be the means of curtailing their visit to the Glens.

In her heart she was certainly rejoiced that they one and all had decided to leave on the morrow.

They were not the sort of people who agree with King Solomon, that the house of mourning is better than the house of feasting!

CHAPTER VIII.

No—she did not wish to be disturbed!

She would have died ten thousand deaths, rather than that any one who might have fathomed her secret, should have come to look upon her or speak to her that night.

Justine was a stupid, simple girl, and might be made to believe that black was white, were such credulity necessary—and therefore Katherine submitted to her ministrations as usual —allowed her even to chafe her icy hands, to bring hot bottles for her feet, to bathe her throbbing temples with some cool essence; and finally, when all these voluntary services had been rendered, to sit beside the bed, and watch the result of her zealous experiments.

"Thank you, Justine, I am better now, and you can go to bed yourself. Don't say how ill I have been again, or papa will hear of it, and forbid my walking at all. Go now, there's a good girl."

Katherine had roused herself to say all this, after she had been in bed—with Justine sitting looking at her—for nearly half an hour.

The girl was really tired and sleepy, and anxious, too, of course, to have a gossip with her fellow-servants about the great events of the evening; so, believing that Miss Katherine would go to sleep as soon as she was left alone, she said good-night, and went away.

And then Katherine rose up—tottering at

every step she made—for her physical weakness was something extraordinary—and, having
locked and bolted the door, threw herself on
the ground (there was to be no soft bed for her
that night), and tried to grapple with the great
misery that had smitten her.

" Dead—dead—dead !"

This was what she kept repeating, with every
variety of intonation, as if the horrible fact itself
could be changed or softened by the changes of
her muffled voice.

Dead !—struck down by some quick and
terrible fever, in the midst of youth, and strength,
and hope. And when, but for her diabolical
jealousy, he might have been living happily in
his own country with the wife he loved, and
with his little child, who was now fatherless.

Dead !—her first and only love—the man
who, had he loved her in return, would have

made this dull earth a paradise for her; nay, would have brought down all her lofty pride, and converted her into a gentle, loving, humble woman.

And now, she had not even the privilege his wife rejoiced in—his wife, who had never loved him as he was worthy of being loved—she had not even the poor privilege of mourning openly for his loss—of showing to the world that she had nothing left to live for, that she gloried in her broken heart, since it was broken for his sake.—No, no—all this was denied her. She must put on a decent black dress for a little while, and it might not be amiss if she even looked gracefully pensive, when friends came to condole with her on her cousin's death, and to say what a pity it was that so fine a young man, so charming a person too, should have been cut off in that shockingly sudden manner.

But beyond this, Katherine must not dare—
she had no right to go.

She was not his widow—not in name at least
—and even *he* had never known what she was
in heart.

      *   *   *   *

Not once had she closed her eyes during that
long, long, awful night. Not one single five
minutes' respite from intense and increasing
anguish, had she obtained. The mind, all worn
as it was with its strife and labour, could find
no place, however narrow, to repose upon—no
place where one ray of light might fall. Had
Katherine never known before, she must have
learnt now what was that " sorrow of the world
that worketh death." She felt, and had no
regret in feeling, that this grief, if it continued,
must kill her. No human strength could stand

out long against it; and hers was already well nigh exhausted.

It had enabled her once or twice during the night to drag herself to the window, and gaze, for a minute or two, at the cold, bright stars, wondering if they contained beings endued with the power of suffering as she was suffering now; but all outward objects, in their calm night aspect, seemed to sicken her very soul, and she soon went back to her crouching attitude on the ground, and to that tearless sobbing, which brought no relief to the over-excited brain.

When the pale dawn came at length into the room, it showed as sad and miserable a spectacle as any dawn had ever looked upon. It showed this proud girl, lying in a strange, crushed-up manner, in the centre of the floor, with hair all training and dishevelled about her, with eyes wide open, and yet seeing no more than if they had been closed; with cheeks as colourless as the white night-dress she had on; and with her whole appearance denoting plainly that some terrible physical crisis had succeeded to the mental agony she had been enduring.

And so, about two hours afterwards, on breaking open her door, they found her.

She had been stricken with catalepsy.

The doctor had two patients in that great house to care of.

They were very differently affected, and required very different treatment. With Miss Wilmot, the thing to be apprehended most, after the first alarming symptoms had been removed, was permanent injury to the brain. She could not shed a single tear, and nothing ever seemed to rouse her from the dull, heavy stupor that oppressed and weighed upon her

from morning till night, and from night till
morning again.

The doctor assured her nearly distracted
parents that this was purely physical, and that
she herself was probably quite unconscious of
suffering. Stronger remedies must be applied—
she had a fine constitution naturally, and could
bear them.

With Ellen it was altogether another affair.

After that first night, when, with the aid of
laudanum, she had slept soundly, she had been
enabled to cry freely—it was considered a bless-
ing for her then, and so perhaps it was ; but,
dating from that morning, she had done nothing
else but cry.   Neither prayers nor threats, neither
kindness nor the reverse, could stop her tears ;
they flowed continually, and with scarcely any
intermission. The doctor said she was crying
herself into the grave as fast as ever she could ;

and they would have sent her home to her friends, had she been in a fit state to travel—but her bodily weakness increased day by day, and she was at length too ill to leave her bed.

About this time, it was judged expedient to have Katherine taken away for entire change of air and scene, at all risks ; so, as the father and mother both decided on accompanying their daughter, they wrote for Mrs. Clavering to come and take care of Ellen in their absence.

They were going to Italy; and if Katherine grew better, would probably remain abroad till the following year—at any rate, through all the spring and summer. Ellen was to consider the Glens her home, for as long as she pleased.

They did not expect, however, that she would live to see them come back ; and they had resolved, in the event of her death, to adopt her little May for their own, being pretty sure that Mrs. Willand would not claim it.

And so, towards the end of the month of April, the family at the Glens divided; those that went, setting out with anxious and sorrowful hearts; she that remained, anticipating nothing but death as a release from her exceeding sorrow and desolation.

It seems so easy and simple a thing to die, when we are in great misery, and so hard and impossible a thing to live on, and endure.

But when death comes quite close to us, and we see his ugly visage, then we feel differently, and are ready to start up and begin fighting the battle of life anew, even if we are sure that we shall get sorely beaten and bruised and wounded again.

Death came very near to Ellen, much nearer than it had ever done before; and when it was standing close beside her, she looked not only at this grim spectre, but into her own heart— and saw that she was unfit to die.

After this, the tide turned.

CHAPTER IX.

ELLEN WILLAND TO NORAH KENNEDY.

" *The Glens, Aug.* 25*th*, 18—.

" MY DEAREST NORAH—

" I never thought to write to you or to any-body else again. It is nearly six months since I have had a pen in my hand, or opened a book, except mechanically, when I have not wanted to be considered obstinate, or unwilling to occupy my mind. Ah me! if people who have suffered hemselves would only look back upon th eir own feelings, they would understand better, I think, how to deal with those who are passing through the waters. What is the use of getting rid of agonising thoughts for a few minutes, when they are sure to indemnify themselves by rushing into the heart again, with a tenfold strength, afterwards? In reply to this, they tell me that even these few minutes of suspension from suffering, is a gain, at least, for the poor body; but I question it. The body is not so quick at gaining what it has lost.

"I promised myself, however, not to write you a gloomy letter—yours to me have been so soothing, so considerate, and so kind—they have really done me good, Norah ; though so different to Mrs. Lane's and Mr. Arnold's. I appreciate them all, and feel very undeserving of the sympathy my great affliction has excited.

"Mamma has written to you of my long

illness, and how she arrived here, and found me
too weak and too indifferent to everything, to
welcome even her—but all this has passed now,
thank God! When they told me I was dying,
really dying, Norah, I was terribly frightened,
notwithstanding that I had from the first been
persuading myself that I desired nothing so much.
Then I made a great effort, fought desperately
with myself, and with my misery, and—recovered. Recovered my bodily health, of course
I mean; for ever to be happy again in this
world, is impossible.

"Had I been with him when he died—my
dear, dear, devoted husband—had I soothed his
last moments, held him in my arms—received
his parting sigh—known that he died believing
and repentant—it would be very, very different
—but as it is!—well, well, I *must* endure it.
God grant me strength and submission.

"I *am* better—my mother and my child have both comforted me. The former has left me now, as Gracie, my brother's wife, has been ailing for some time; and mamma was wanted there. She would have taken me with her, but I refused to go—in the first place because I felt it would be anguish unspeakable to look upon the scenes where Sydney and myself first met and loved each other, and in the second place because Mr. Wilmot writes me word that they are coming home next month, and that he should be greatly disappointed at not finding me here on their return. Katherine is better, but so changed, he says, quite the old woman in her looks, and very uncertain and irritable in her temper. She talks a good deal about May, and seems anxious to have the child with her again. This is one reason why they are coming home.

"I do not expect to stay here very much longer, however, now. I mean to try and earn my own living—we have nothing, you know, not a farthing, now my dear Sydney has been taken from us, and I *must* have the means of educating his daughter like a lady. Perhaps they will offer to adopt her—the family at the Glens—but she is all my comfort, and I cannot give her up.

"You have no idea what a quiet, monotonous life I am leading at present. I never see a creature besides the servants, and never go out beyond the grounds. It is true the weather is too warm for walking, and I have no inclination to use their carriages or horses.

"Mr. Mervyn has been back a long time. I have not seen him, of course, but he is just as kind as ever, sending me books, and flowers, and fruit, continually—sometimes bringing them himself. I think perhaps I ought to see him just once, to thank him for his attentions, which even you, Norah, must acknowledge to be disinterested, coming from him to me. I must leave off writing for to-day, because I feel one of my fits of overpowering depression—(when the whole earth grows black as midnight)—stealing slowly but surely over me. I will try to finish my letter to-morrow.

"September 7th.—I have been indolent, wholly and entirely indolent, which means that I have done actually nothing for more than a week. It has been a very trying week to me, not only on account of unusual depression, but in consequence of continual nervous headaches, which are new to me in the degree that I have been afflicted with them now. One day, when the pain had almost maddened me, I walked down the front avenue to see if there was more breeze in that direction than at the back of the house ; and who should I meet, a few yards from the entrance gates, but Mr. Mervyn, carrying a large packet of books, and a bouquet of flowers. I assure you, Norah, I would have given kingdoms, had I possessed them, to have avoided him at that moment, feeling ill, and stupified, and miserable as I did ; but of course it was impossible, so we shook hands. I told him what a dreadful headache I had got, and he went back to the house with me, and made me order a cup of very strong coffee, which did me good almost immediately. Then I thanked him for all his kindness, admired the beautiful flowers he had now brought, and confessed that I had not been able to read a line since my great trouble. I could see that he *really* sympathised

with me, sympathised as only those *can* do who
have gone through the same sort of trial; and
I am not ashamed to say that this was very
sweet and soothing to me. Think, dear Norah,
how lonely I am! how sad it is day after day
to keep all my gloomy and bitter thoughts to
myself—how the old yearning has to be for
ever stifled and repressed, because I know that
it cannot again in this world be satisfied. No,
believe me, I do not expect, I do not even *wish*
to find again a love like Sydney's—that would·
be impossible; but surely friendship need not be
denied me. I cannot long exist without affection
of some kind, and at present I have no inclination (for reasons I have told you of) to return
amongst those dear ones, who would bestow it
on me in ample measure. If you knew Mr.
Mervyn, there would be no necessity for my
assuring you that I should be perfectly safe in

accepting friendship from him. He is cold, calm, intellectual, and a little proud. He reminds me of the stars on a winter's night: you can look up to and admire them, but it never occurs to you that there is any warmth in their brightness, or that they would come down to warm *you* if there *was*. To prove, however, that I am quite frank and open with you, I will confess that had I known him years and years ago, when my heart was free, and my nature full of romance, he is just the sort of man whom I should probably have fallen in love with, and worshipped in a very unreasonable and ridiculous manner; but now—oh if I could only convince you how safe and sure I feel now, you would smile at the solemn caution you once gave me. I have not seen him since that first day, and from something he said, I don't expect he will call again until the family return.   In my next letter you will doubtless be informed of their arrival.

"Yours ever affectionately,

"ELLEN WILLAND."

CHAPTER X.

ELLEN WILLAND TO NORAH KENNEDY.

" *The Glens, December 7th,* 18—.

" DEAREST NORAH,—

" The truly affectionate interest you continue to express in all that concerns me, and your anxiety to know what is going on here at present, have roused me at last to begin a letter, of which I shall write a few lines whenever I have an opportunity of doing so—a thing of much rarer occurrence than it used to be, I assure you.

"The family arrived at the Glens the first week in October, all tired of their wanderings, and professedly delighted at getting home again. I was very much shocked when I first saw Katherine—she looked so old and thin, and her hair, in some parts, had become quite grey. But they seemed to think her wonderfully better, and when I asked her concerning her health, she replied, shortly and coldly, that she was quite well. Mrs. Wilmot scarcely ever leaves her daughter for a moment, and so they have given me the housekeeping to attend to, and this occupies pretty nearly every moment of my time. My little daughter appears much less mine than Aunt Katherine's; and as the child is an immense comfort to her, I should not particularly object to this monopoly, if it were not that I see May's affections being fast weaned from me—her mother, who has nothing else to love—in favour of one who loads her with presents and caresses, and makes her on all occasions a first object. As for myself, it is evident that Katherine cannot even see me without getting painfully excited ; it must be something more than mere common hatred that she feels. I spoke of this once to Mr. Wilmot, who was much affected, and told me that they feared her brain was not quite in a healthy state —that she had conceived the strange idea that Sydney's death was owing to her having urged her father to procure him that appointment at Guatemala. Poor girl! and this is why Mrs. Wilmot is afraid to leave her, and why they like her to have May constantly with her. Of course, under these circumstances, I have nothing to say ; but it is very bitter to feel that I am losing the first place in my child's affections. And oh, Norah, my life is dreary ! dreary !

Very few people come to see us now, for Katherine's strange state is everywhere known, and
it causes the house to be avoided. Mr. Mervyn
is, however, an exception, and indeed if it were
not for him, I don't really know how I should
endure so miserable an existence as mine. He
sees it all, pities, and tries to console me. I
think Katherine has taken a dislike to him, for
she is always more irritable and disagreeable
when he is here, than on ordinary occasions.
He will come to-night—he told me so last time
he was here, and I have been looking forward
to it ever since. I cannot help it, Norah, I am
so very, very desolate!

    " December 11th.—Such a scene since I
wrote the last few lines of my letter! and now
I am going away. I have quite made up my
mind, and nothing will turn me from it. Judge
whether I could do otherwise. Mr. Mervyn

came to spend the evening with us, as he had promised, and, as usual after he had talked a little with Mr. and Mrs. Wilmot, he devoted himself entirely to me. It was nothing new, and nobody had ever remarked upon it, or seemed to think it strange before. No sooner had he gone, however, than Katherine, in her mother's presence, (Mr. Wilmot had walked down the avenue with our guest), began to rail at me in the most unmeasured language, accused me of the grossest indelicacy in flirting so shamelessly before I had left off my widow's weeds, called Mr Mervyn all the injurious names she could think of, and finally declared, that if I meant to go on dishonouring my husband's memory in 'that way,' she hoped I would do it elsewhere, and not in the very sight of his relatives, who felt themselves insulted, and set at open defiance by such conduct!

" I was literally so astonished, Norah, that I had no power to say a single word in reply. I believe I grew very pale, for Mrs. Wilmot (who was looking quite distressed), exclaimed suddenly,—' You had better go to bed, Ellen, I am sure you are tired;' and knowing now that if I spoke at all, it would be in language that I had no right to use to one so unfortunate as Katherine, I took the hint, and hurried away to my own room.

" Since this, Katherine has never met me, even accidentally, without gathering into her sharpened features all the cont mpt they are capable of expressing, and I live in daily, hourly dread of Mr. Mervyn's next visit."

" December 20th.—I have been so busy with my preparations for getting away, that till now I have not found a moment for continuing my letter. I don't think I told you that I had

decided on going *secretly*. I am certain they
would never consent to it, or that at least the
opposition would be so strong, that my resolution would falter ; and I *must* go—I feel that on
all accounts it is far, far better. I have been
much happier, much more satisfied with myself
since I have finally determined on my course of
action.   For a long time I was quite undecided
where to go,—St. Ives being out of the question,
as I mean to earn my own living.—Poor mamma has enough to do to keep herself, and help
Maurice.   Well, in this dilemma, I chanced one
day to find, amongst some old papers, the address of Miss Jane, you remember our dear
Miss Jane, in Paris?   I got it from Gertrude
Lomond, nearly two years ago, when Miss Jane
had just commenced school-keeping, on her own
accounts, in the Avenue Marbœuf, at Paris.   So
I decided at once on going straight to her.   If

her school is prospering, she may herself be able to employ me for singing and drawing, at any rate, for the first, and if not, she will help me to get pupils. I have fortunately enough money for my journey, and to keep me a few weeks, even if I fail in immediately obtaining employment. My greatest trial is leaving May, my little blue-eyed darling; but it would be too selfish to take her from her present home, until I have another prepared for her. She will be well cared for here, and her nurse, who is in my secret, has promised to write me constant accounts of her. So now, dear Norah, you know all my plans, and I venture to hope that *for once* you will commend me—a little.

"I have not written to Miss Jane, because I remember what a very prudent little body it was, and if she saw no certain prospect of my earning a livelihood, she might throw cold water

L 2

upon the scheme altogether, which would only
distress me without in the least affecting my
resolution.   I never allow myself to *think* now.
I must learn to be cold, practical, matter-of-fact,
unsentimental.   I have got to fight with a world
where I know these qualifications are indispensable.   I hope to become something else too,
besides all this, but what it is, *you* will not care
to hear ; and alas ! I am still very, very far from
anything of the sort, notwithstanding my great
trials.   Think of me, dear Norah, about this
day-week, when I hope to be in Paris—the
Paris I have not seen since the old, bright days,
when you and I were young.   You will start at
this, but I am not young any longer, whatever
you may be.   In looks as well as in heart, I am
old and faded—Miss Jane will not recognize me,
that is certain, and oh how trying to me will
our first meeting be.   The last day I had any

conversation with her was the day of our brilliant concours, do you remember it? Ah, I
know you do, and the little room where you
told me your early history. I can see you now,
sitting on the ground, surrounded by your old
letters, looking so pale and excited, so wholly
indifferent to all the present vanities with which
my giddy head was filled. Oh Norah, Norah,
I must not think, I dare not look back. What
a wondrous, wondrous thing is this mortal life
of ours, promising so much and giving so little,
to some, and to others promising nothing and
giving all. Is it not Tennyson who
says,—

> ' *There's something in our lives amiss,*
> *Will be unriddled by and bye?'*

and yet I doubt whether Tennyson himself
had any suspicion of the *real* wisdom contained
in those lines when he wrote them.

" I must say good bye, dear Norah, my time here now is so very short.

                    " Yours ever affectionately,

                              " NELLY."

" P.S. I have not seen Mr. Mervyn since the eveniug I told you of, and I am glad. They will give him what explanation they please of my flight. I shall leave a letter for Mr. Wilmot, telling him why I go. I don't think he willl blame me."

CHAPTER XI.

IT was the last day of the old year, a bitterly cold, bright morning, when Ellen Willand, having arrived in Paris only the night before, and slept at a small hotel near the Northern railway, (because she felt too ill and exhausted to get farther,) set out on foot to find her old friend in the Champs Elysées. She had of course no idea of the distance; but even had it been otherwise, her journey had cost her so much more than she had reckoned on, that her scanty purse would have inclined her to make

the effort, rather than incur the additional ex-
pense of coach-hire.

And yet she was feeling very weak, and wholly
unfit for exertion of any kind.

Her timid, and essentially dependent nature,
had done extraordinary violence to itself, in
forming and keeping the resolution of taking
this long journey alone, and without either the
knowledge or consent of any one interested in
her.   The mental conflict it had entailed (to say
nothing of the actual fatigue she had endured,
travelling in the cheapest way, and at so severe a
season of the year), had done its work upon her
frail body, and she had felt, on arriving the previous evening, as if some dreadful illness were
coming on, which would speedily terminate all
her struggles and wanderings.

But a tolerably good night had so far changed
the aspect of affairs, that Ellen decided, on

awakening in the morning, to find her way to Miss Jane's at all risks. It seemed such a terrible thing to be without a single friend or acquaintance in all this great city—she who, when she was last here, had been the darling of so many hearts, and with such a bright, sunny future before her.

There was one good point in her present almost desperate circumstances, in her diminished purse, and in her sensations of physical weakness—they kept her from thinking of the • past as gloomily and exclusively as she might have done, had not the actual difficulties and distress that threatened her, engrossed her mind, as she walked rapidly—too rapidly for her strength—along the crowded and glittering Paris streets, on that bright, freezing morning.

In the end, she was obliged, though with extreme reluctance, to take a citadine, and to desire the man to drive her as fast as he could to the address she gave him.

The symptoms of approaching illness had all returned, and poor Ellen felt every minute an hour until she could reach somebody who knew her, and who would advise her what to do.

At last they arrived at the house. Everything about here was so strangely familiar, was connected with so many associations of the past, that Ellen had resolutely closed her eyes, and only opened them when the vehicle drew up, with a sudden jerk, before a large *port cochère,* and the man asked her from his seat if that was right.

" Quite right. Let me get out."

She got out, paid the fare, and was left standing alone in the comparatively quiet road.

The next thing was to ring the porter's bell, and enquire for her friend. She did not know on which floor Miss Jane held her school, or whether her pupils were boarders, and she lived here altogether.

The man appeared, looking surly enough, for he had been disturbed at his midday meal.

" Mademoiselle H—. Is she here ?"

" No."

He was returning to his lodge.

" But she lives here, does she not ? She has a school for young ladies."

Ellen's heart was beating so rapidly that she could scarcely say even this.

" She has left Paris this three months. You can ascend *au troisième*."

It was a mercy she did not faint then and there ; but if she had done so, the surly porter would not have stayed to see it. His soup was getting cold, and it was not his business to answer questions about old lodgers ; so having delivered his last piece of information, he went back to his dinner, and shut the door.

And Ellen, not knowing why or wherefore, but in simple desperation, and because she could not tell what else to do, began the arduous ascent *au troisième*.

She had to rest continually, and to press her hand tightly to her side, which was aching dreadfully, and adding to those other sensations of illness that she must still fight against, till at least she could find some refuge, some quiet spot where she might lay down her poor, throbbing head, and die if needs be, or at any rate get a temporary respite from the overpowering misery she was feeling now.

In answer to her timid ring at the first door she came to, on the third story, a young lady of mild and prepossessing appearance presented herself, and inquired courteously the object of

Ellen's visit—did she wish to see either of
the pupils?

"No. I am a stranger here. I came in
search of an old friend of mine, Miss H—.
The porter told me she had left, but said I
might get further information from somebody
on this floor. I am sorry to have disturbed
you."

"Not in the least, I assure you. You look
very tired. Will you walk in and rest for a few
minutes in my little salon? The children are in
their recreation just now, and perhaps I can give
you the information you require."

Grateful beyond description for these kind
words, and this unexpected civility from a
stranger, Ellen accepted the invitation, and was
soon seated in a delicious *fauteuil*, by a pleasant
little wood fire, and with a *chaufrette* under
her poor, half-frozen feet.

"And now," said the young lady, drawing her own chair to the fire, and looking compassionately at her pale guest—" what can I tell yon about your friend? you had not heard of her marriage?"

" Her marriage—no ; I had no idea—the truth is, I have never met her, or had any correspondence with her, since my school days —but I heard that she had a school herself here now, and I have come a long, long way, in the hope of finding her, and obtaining her assistance in getting pupils."

" I am very sorry.   It was unfortunate you did not write.   But you spoke of your school days—were you educated in Paris?"

" Yes, at Madame Guillemar's, in the Faubourg St. Honoré.   Miss Jane was there with her pupil, Valerie Jocelyn."

" And you—forgive me if I am impertinent —you are Ellen Clavering ?"

" I was—" and poor Ellen glanced at her black dress, while burning tears rushed to her eyes.

The young lady understood it all in a moment, and was unspeakably distressed.

" Ah, *mon Dieu ! que je suis bête.* I beseech you to pardon me. I was so excited at the thought of your being the Miss Clavering of whom I have heard so much—you had been • so often described to me. You must know that I too was a pupil at Madame Guillemar's— after your time, of course—and having made Miss Jane's acquaintance there, she sought me out on taking this school, and I became her assistant. When she so unexpectedly gave it up to be married, the pupils were transferred to me; but it does not answer very well; and I have another project in view at present."

"But Miss Jane?" said Ellen, greatly interested in what she had been hearing—"whom did she marry? we used to think her old maidism quite a settled point."

The young schoolmistress smiled. "So she always declared herself, but destiny had something better in store for her. After Valerie's marriage, her father, who had fretted himself into a low, nervous state of health, renewed the offer he had, it appears, made years before to Miss Jane. *Then* she had refused him, because she knew his family would be so indignant at his marrying a poor, English governess; but in his sorrow and desolation, her warm, kind heart could not turn from his pleadings (I believe he had always been fond of her), and so he came one day and took her off; and I hear from her that they are very, very happy."

" I am glad of it—she was a dear, good little woman, and deserved the reward she has found —where are they living ?"

" At Tours—and she wants me, after the Easter vacation, to go and settle there, assuring me of success, either with a school like this, or in giving private lessons."

Ellen sighed deeply. She was thinking of her own disappointment now, and of her utterly friendless position. Her new acquaintance seemed fearful of asking questions, and yet quite ready to bestow her sympathy, if it might be accepted.

" You would like Madame Jocelyn's address, perhaps—or shall I write and tell her of your visit ?"

" Thank you very much. I will take the

address, but——" she paused—then, after a moment—" do you know whether Madame Guillemar is still living here ?"

" Ah, the poor woman, she is dead. The school is still going on, but I am not acquainted with the lady who keeps it."

Her last hope gone !—Her brain seemed spinning round ; but she had no longer an excuse for staying here. The recreation must be finished, and the pupils waiting for their mistress.

Ellen rose.

" I am exceedingly indebted to you for your kindness. If I remain in Paris, I will see you again."

" I shall be delighted. In the meanwhile, if I can do anything for you—I have a few friends here—will you give me your address ?"

Ellen coloured painfully. " I have no address

at present. Last night I slept at the nearest
hotel to the station—I was so ill and tired. If
I stay, I must have a lodging."

"Shall I look out for one for you?"

" You are very good, I shall be greatly obliged ;
but I must first decide as to my plans. I expect
to find letters at the post office. Stay, here is
the name of the place I am at now—but if I
am well enough, I will come to you again to-
morrow or the next day."

" And should I not see you I will send or
come to you."

" Thank you a thousand times. Good
morning."

" Adieu, *chère madame*—I do hope I may
be of use to you."

So they parted! and Ellen, more dead than
alive, bent her steps in the direction of the post

office to which she had left word with her child's
nurse to address her letters.

There was one for her in Mr. Wilmot's
handwriting, but she dared not open it till she
reached home. Should it contain anything
agitating or distressing, Ellen felt sure it would
put the finishing stroke to her state of bodily
weakness, and then what would become of
her ?

She had not tasted food since she left the
hotel in the morning, and the short, winter day
was already closing in. There was no resource
but to take another citadine, and to get home
(alas, what a home !) as fast as she could.

"Candles, a little tea, and some bread and
butter," these were what she ordered to be
brought to her room as soon as she arrived.
The yearning for rest, for quiet, for the privilege
of weeping torrents of tears over her miserable,

miserable desolation, had become intense, and must be indulged if she were to retain even her reason.

There was a good fire laid ready for lighting, but it was not until a succession of violent shivering fits warned her of the peril she was running, that Ellen ventured on applying a match to the dry chips, and filling the cold, dreary-looking room with a warm, bright blaze.

By this time her frugal meal was waiting for her, and having hastily swallowed a cup of hot though wretchedly weak, poor tea, she drew the candles nearer to her, and prepared to read her letters.

For there were two, one enclosed in the other, the second in a writing with which she was quite unfamiliar, and which was carelessly laid aside until Mr. Wilmot's few lines should have been perused.

This was his letter—

"MY DEAR ELLEN,

"I am sincerely grieved that you should have thought it necessary to take so decided a step as that of leaving our protection, and the home you had here, in the clandestine way you have done. I am aware that you had much to put up with, but so you will have, my poor child, in almost any position you may succeed in obtaining, and you are far too young to go about the world alone. I am full of anxiety when I think of you; but Mrs. W— and Kate are so indignant at your conduct, that, at present, I cannot urge you to return. When you are settled anywhere, send me your address, and I will enclose you some money; this, at least, you will find indispensable wherever you may be. But you have acted foolishly, Ellen, and on the

impulse of the moment. You should have remembered that you had always one friend here,
who, as far as he could, would have shielded you
from unkindness and unjustice. For your child
you need have no anxiety, she is the great person
in the house at present.

" I depend upon hearing from you speedily—
do not allow a false delicacy to hinder you from
writing.

" Yours, always sincerely and affectionately,

" JAMES WILMOT."

Ellen cried so much over this letter, (which
made her view her own conduct in such a totally
different light from that in which she had
hitherto regarded it), that her other letter was
for awhile quite forgotten; and it only struck
her afterwards, that Mr. Wilmot had enclosed it
without a single remark of any kind.

These were the contents, startling and agitating enough, you may well believe.

" MY DEAR FRIEND,

"For I hope, under any circumstances, you will permit me so to call you—I am going to venture on something which I almost fear may put your friendship to too severe a test, and you must have a little patience with me if I am tedious, and even prosy, in my manner of doing it. But let me first tell you how deeply shocked and distressed I was on going to the Glens yesterday, (to see *you* chiefly—this, at any rate, you know)—to find that the bird had flown, the poor drooping bird, that I had so long been watching with interest and compassion. And now, as friendship has its privileges, and you are sure that I *am* your friend, permit me to say that I think the step you have taken is unworthy of yourself; I cannot condemn it more severely. You have given pain to more than you know, or perhaps care to know of, in leaving, Scotland so abruptly and mysteriously. At your age any honourable protection is better than going forth into the world friendless and alone; and I may add, that I believe it would be utterly impossible to find a person so wholly unfitted as yourself, for the warfare you have undertaken. You know it as well as I do. I must not, however, weary or make you impatient before I come to that point of my letter which will demand all your indulgence. I fear to write it, my pen trembles over the paper, as if it knew and felt the audacity to which it is to be made a party. And I should be so truly and unspeakably grieved, either to wound you, or lose your friendship.

" So let me say in the beginning, that no

living man can have a more profound sympathy
with the affliction you have recently endured, a
more profound respect for all the tender memories connected with that affliction, than myself. A kindred sorrow has invested me with
the right and the power to express thus much;
and it comes from my heart—you may believe
it.

"Will it seem strange to you, if I add that
it has been this very perfection of sympathy,
arising out of our mutual loneliness, that has
created in me the strong desire to promote your
happiness by devoting my life to the task?
Pray understand me. I do not mean to say in
broad, coarse terms, ' Will you be my wife?' and
ask for an immediate straightforward ' yes' or
' no.' This, in your position, would be both
shocking and indelicate, and might justly alienate
you from me for ever. I only mean to place

the idea gently before you, that you may, by degrees, and without outraging any feelings and memories that ought to be sacred, look at it kindly and indulgently—perhaps, in the end, with pleasure. Do not fancy, though, that I feel too confident, or presume on the friendly relations already established between us. I presume on nothing, I expect little, and unless you should ultimately be *quite* convinced that the uniting of our destinies would secure *your* happiness, I would not for the whole universe have you entertain my proposition. Think of it calmly, dispassionately, with all your *judgment* employed in the matter. Remember the points of dissimilarity in our characters, my love of study, and interest in many things that I scarcely think now, after all you have suffered, you would like to take the trouble to understand, and then the absence, in me, of those religious feelings, or principles if you prefer it, that appear to you of so much importance. Think, I repeat, my dear friend, of all these things, against which you have only to weigh the facts of my sincere affection for you, and my earnest desire—it *is* earnest, Ellen—to devote my life to your happiness. I will not ask you to write to me yet, whatever your impression of this letter may be ; but at the end of six months from the present date, let me, by some means or other, learn where you may be found, and I will come and receive your answer from your own lips. Till then, adieu.

     " Yours, under all circumstances,

         " Faithfully and truly,

            " GERALD MERVYN."

It took a long time to get to the end of this

singular love-letter—longer on account of the exceeding dimness of Ellen's eyes, and the tumultuous beating of her heart as she read. To give any clear account of the wild torrent of thoughts and emotions that swept over her mind, excited as it already was, by the fever of her body, would be simply impossible; but amongst them all, and standing out foremost, it must be told, was an unnatural, delirious kind of joy, at the idea of once more being loved, and sheltered, and petted, as she had used to be.

This was the instinctive out-gushing of that germ of selfishness in her character which has been before alluded to, and which was, no doubt, increased just now by that physical weakness that would soon prostrate her mind altogether.

And then she had felt so wholly, utterly desolate in this strange place, so like a wilful child, who, having wandered from its home, and become lost amongst strangers, eagerly stretches out its little arms to the first friendly voice it hears.

If he, Gerald Mervyn, the writer of that letter, which seemed almost to have turned her poor, tired brain, could have presented himself before Ellen Willand at that moment, there is no doubt that she would have stretched out her arms childishly and innocently, and asked for the love he offered, more humbly and pleadingly than he had asked for hers.

But he was not there, she was all alone; and after reading again and again, till all the sweet words danced before her failing sight, the letter in which she saw only unequalled goodness and nobility of heart, Ellen crept to her cold bed, and suffered anew, in hideous and fantastic dreams, the miseries and anxieties of the last few wretched days.

CHAPTER XII.

IT was still cold, very cold, though not quite the cold of mid-winter, in Paris, when one morning the churlish porter in the Avenue Marbœuf was again summoned from his lodge, to answer an enquiry for Mademoiselle H———.

He had sent away no end of letters addressed to her, or to her care, within the last few weeks; and at this fresh application, which he chose to consider as a personal insult, he only growled out the two words "*Au troisième*," and with a scowl that would have alarmed any less intrepid

individual than the one standing so quietly before him, retired to his den to find consolation
in the fumes of some execrable tobacco, that
made the lady cough as she hurried past his
inhospitable dwelling.

Fortunately, she was able to run up the three
flights of stairs much more nimbly than poor
Ellen Willand, a few weeks ago, had done; and
then, ringing at the bell on the third story, she
was answered by the same pleasant-looking
personage who had appeared on that former
occasion.

" Does not Mademoiselle H—— reside here ?"

"Not now—she is married and gone away.
I am the present mistress of the school she kept
here."

There was a quickness and an abruptness
about the manner of the enquirer, that seemed
to demand brief, straightforward answers.

But she looked puzzled, and a good deal put out, by this unexpected reply—

"Did you wish particularly to see Madame Jocelyn?"

The lady started, and then smiled a little to herself. She remembered the name, and her thoughts went back to a certain tea-party in Miss Jane's private room long, long ago. But recovering almost immediately her presence of mind, she said, as abruptly as at first—

"No—I want Mrs. Willand, who came to Paris about five weeks ago, on purpose to find Miss Jane. I have written repeatedly to this address, and receiving no answers to my letters, I became anxious, and—and so I am here."

The other could scarcely give her time to finish this explanation.

"Oh how thankful I am!" she exclaimed, clasping her hands, and showing a countenance full of emotion. " Come in, and I will tell you all about her. Poor thing, poor thing !"

Norah, for of course it *was* Norah, eagerly followed her amiable conductress into the same neat little *salon* in which Ellen had sat on the miserable day of her coming here; and the young lady, after briefly relating that visit and its bitter disappointment, thus continued her story :—

" I told you it had been settled between us, that if, on the second day, I saw nothing of your friend, I should go or send to the hotel where she had been staying. I was afraid, very much afraid, that she would suffer from the fatigue and excitement she had so evidently gone through—her whole manner and appearance indicated approaching illness ; and so, on the third morning after her visit—it was fortunately Sunday, and therefore a holiday for me

—I started early, and arrived about noon at the address she had given me. Judge of my feelings when I was told, in answer to my enquiries for the young English lady, that she had been seized, the day but one after her arrival, with violent rheumatic fever, and was now lying in a very precarious and doubtful state indeed. Of course I went upstairs immediately, my heart full of pity for the poor young thing who had seemed so friendless and unhappy. In her room I found one of our sisters of charity, whom the people at the hotel had called in to nurse her, and through whose care everything had been made neat and comfortable about her. I think, however, there is little doubt that she had slept on damp sheets the first two nights; and this had decided the character of her illness, though in any case an illness of some kind she *must* have had. I should have said that a doctor

had also been summoned, when the first alarming
symptoms betrayed themselves, and that at the
time I found her, every possible attention had
been paid to the case, and everything done that
could be done to avert its most serious consequences.

" Still, in spite of all, there was then great
danger, and the kind sister and myself were in
despair at the poor dear lady's friendless position.   We could find no letters or papers
containing the names or addresses of any persons in England: it is true there was a small
desk on her table, but unless all hope of saving
life had been over, we did not feel justified in
breaking this open ; and she must have lost or
hidden her keys, for we could never find them.
The delirium lasted nine days, during which her
life hung upon a thread ; but at the end of that
time the strong remedies prevailed, and, God

be praised! she has since then been surely, though very, very slowly, recovering. I have not been able to see her often, but on my last visit she was composed enough to dictate to me a few lines to some friend—an uncle I believe, in Scotland—making the best of this terrible illness, and telling him that, as soon as she was quite well, she should either return to her own relations, or pursue her original plans in this country.

"Alas! you will find her wofully changed— a mere wreck even of what she was on her arrival, when, in spite of great delicacy of appearance, there was sufficient beauty remaining to enable me to guess that my visitor was the fair and pretty Ellen Clavering that Miss Jane, and all the girls at Madame Guillemar's, used to talk so much about."

"Poor Nelly!" said Norah, who had listened to this long account with an emotion she could hardly restrain, " what a succession of trials her life has been—*I* must take care of her now."

" You are not related to her ?" asked the young Frenchwoman, who had been examining Norah rather curiously, and trying to remember whether she answered to the description she had received of any of the other English girls at Madame Guillemar's.

"No. I was at school with her; we were great friends, and I have formed no new ties that might have helped me to forget old friendships."

Mademoiselle looked again at her *vis-à-vis*, and wondered still more. Surely this could not be the unattractive, eccentric Irish girl, whom they all spoke of as Ellen Clavering's bosom-friend—this graceful, self-possessed, and rather handsome young lady.

But Norah's manner, though strictly polite, and even agreeable, was not encouraging to curiosity—so her hostess asked no questions, but returned to the subject of Ellen's illness.

"I forgot to say that in the beginning I wrote a full account of all that had occurred to Madame Jocelyn, who was deeply distressed at my recital, and would have come to Paris herself, but that Monsieur was laid up at the time with some passing illness, and demanded all her care. She sent me money for Madame Willand's use till she should get better, because I had told her frankly that I feared the lady was without present resources ; and the people of the hotel were evidently anxious on the subject."

Norah looked annoyed.

" Can she not be removed into apartments in a better part of the town ?"

"Oh not yet, it would not be safe. These rheumatic fevers are such tedious, wearying maladies ; and then, poor dear, I daresay her continued depression of spirits has diminished the chances of a quick recovery. She will get well much faster now you are come."

" I hope so ; will you give me the address at once ? I need not detain you longer."

The address was written out.

" As Ellen's friend, you must allow me to thank you earnestly and sincerely for the kindness you have shown her," said Norah in taking leave ; she had hitherto been too full of Ellen herself, to remember what was due to this really good Samaritan. " You will come and see us, I hope, whenever you can."

" I will indeed."

" Good-bye then now. I am all impatience to get to Ellen."

She ran down stairs even faster than she had come up, desired the driver of the coach in waiting for her, not to spare his horses for this once, but to make all possible speed to the place she told him of. And then, leaning back and doubling her thick veil over her face, she cried long and heartily over the troubles of her dear Nelly—her poor, widowed, desolate little friend.

*　　*　　*　　*　　*

" It seems still all like a dream to me, Norah. I cannot realize it. I shall be afraid to go to sleep to-night, lest in the morning, when I awake, I shall find you gone."

" No fear of that, my child. As long as you want me, if it is to the end of one of our lives, I will never leave you. I am my own mistress now, as I told you."

" Your own mistress ?—I forget how, I am still so very weak, Norah."

" You are indeed, and must neither talk nor listen much at one time. I explained to you that my father has married again, and given me my portion to do what I like with—that is all."

" Oh yes, but you will like it. You were always fond of liberty and independence. How very, very good of you to come to me. I have been so, *so* lonely."

" I know, but you are not to dwell upon that any longer, Nelly, it is over, over for ever,

I hope; and as soon as you are well enough, we will go and travel together. I must have a chaperone you see, and your matronship will constitute you a very efficient one, and enable us to do all sorts of wild and delightful things, without the least fear of getting talked about— not that *I* should mind if we were."

Ellen smiled faintly.

" The same Norah that used to sit with her feet hanging out of the bed-room window— only, grown so very handsome, that I have still my doubts as to her identity. Norah the great Poetess too—how strange it all seems !"

" Well, my child, I give you leave to think of me as much as you please—as Norah, the ugly school-girl ; or Norah, the handsome young lady ; or Miss Kennedy, the renowned poetess ! anything you like, so long as it *is* me, and not yourself. You have been thinking quite too much of yourself this long time."

" I suppose I have, but it was inevitable in my wretched circumstances. Now I feel such a sweet, full, perfect sense of protection and safety again, that my brain aches in trying to realize it, so as to feel sure it is not a dream."

" After a good night you will have no difficulty in settling the point to your satisfaction. Now I am going to make some tea for us both, for you must know I have been fasting all day, and you are to lie quiet—quiet as a good little mouse, and watch me in my labours. Then I shall bring this small, and, I fear, somewhat ricketty table to your bedside, and we will have a cosy meal together. Dear, dear Nelly! if you only knew how happy I am in being here and in taking care of you."

Ellen's rest that night was such as to satisfy both the doctor and nurses, that her progress henceforth would be as rapid as they all desired.

CHAPTER XIII.

It was the mingling of various feelings and emotions that induced Ellen Willand, during all those long, bright, summer wanderings with Norah, to keep her one secret from the knowledge or suspicion of the latter. In all but this, her heart was laid bare to her friend, who listened to whatever it pleased Ellen to talk about, and sympathised with every hope and fear, as cordially and self-forgetfully as she had done in the old days at school.

For Norah, whether from nature or the circumstances of her life, was not only unselfish
(which loving characters often are), but essentially unegotistical, which is a much rarer thing.
She never wanted to talk about herself at all ;
and thus poor Nelly was once more in danger
of having her greatest failing encouraged, and
her weaknesses ministered to, when she ought
to have been gaining strength for the new con-
flicts that were before her.

In the beginning, and while she was still
almost a helpless invalid on Norah's hands, Ellen
had accepted all the petting and indulgence,
which the other was only too disposed to lavish
upon her, as a matter of course ; and as health
and strength returned, it did not occur to her
that there was any necessity for changing the
established order of things between them.   It
was so pleasant to be once more the object of

tender care and watchfulness ; it reminded her so much of her brief married life, that she could almost believe Sydney's spirit had taken posses- sion of Norah's form for the sake of resuming its old ministerings of affection ; and though she knew and felt how immeasurably she was the debtor of this true and faithful Friend, there was too much genuine and enthusiastic *love* in the spirit of Norah's kindness, for any oppressive sense of obligation to be laid upon the mind of the Receiver.

And then it must also be acknowledged, as a little excuse for Ellen's careless acceptance of so much that she never seemed to repay at this time, that her thoughts, generally, were intensely preoccupied.

The period was fast approaching when she should have to give an answer to that letter which she knew so thoroughly now, that the words, some or other of them, were always shining in golden characters before her sight. Whether she was walking, driving, sailing, or sitting still, whether it was night or day, the early dawn or the shadowy twilight, there they were, like the spirits of some lost or absent friends, from whom we feel we are only separated *bodily*. It is not given to every one to express just *themselves* in what they write, but Mr. Mervyn had contrived to do so in Ellen's idea at least; and this it was that made the words of his letter seem always like a familiar presence, whose haunting of us we esteem our greatest joy.

At first, that is, immediately after her long illness, she had tried very resolutely so to discipline her thoughts that they should not dwell oftener on this friend of hers, than on any other subject connected with the past. She had seen

clearly *then*, that whatever advantages a union
with Gerald Mervyn might appear to offer, there
were weighty reasons why she ought not to
entertain the idea of it for a moment. First
and foremost his want of religious prin-
ciple.

This, he himself had the honesty and the
courage to set before her. *He* felt that it
might come as a cloud between their affection
for each other; *she* knew that it must, sooner
or later, be destructive to her own happiness
and peace of mind.

And so she had assured herself then, while
the alarm-note to a re-awakened conscience still
sounded in her ear, that, cost what it might,
she would, when the time came, firmly decline
the brilliant destiny offered to her acceptance.
She would open her heart fully and unreservedly
to the friend who had nobly urged her to be

cautious in making a decision; and they would be friends still, and for ever.

Perhaps, had Ellen remained alone, with her Bible and her conscience for advisers, she might have had strength to keep this laudable resolution, and to close her ears to the voice of the Charmer. But her life's discipline was to be worked out in another way.

Was it wonderful, that the sunny land of Italy, the companionship of a gifted woman whose only God was nature, and the constant reading with her of books where human genius alone made its presence felt, should call into active life that dangerous imagination, which, once allowed the reins, would be sure to carry its victim whithersoever it listed !

In a few plain words, however, it may be told and understood, that Ellen suffered her prepossession in favour of Mr. Mervyn to grow into an absorbing attachment, which gained strength from its concealment, as well as from her own perfect conviction, that by gratifying it, she would place all her earthly happiness, perhaps even her eternal salvation, in most fearful jeopardy.

But she loved him—she was a weak woman— and what could rescue her from her fate?

Blame her as much as you like for all this— trample upon her in your righteous indignation —but still do her justice.

Sydney was not forgotten. His memory was as dear to her now as it had been in the first hour she knew she was a widow ; she thought indeed that it was Mr. Mervyn's generous allowance of, and sympathy with her unavoidable regrets, that had chiefly endeared him to her. But, it must be remembered, Ellen had never found in her husband anything like the realization of her Ideal. She had loved him gratefully, tenderly, faithfully ; but she had not fashioned him into an idol to be worshipped ; and until a woman does this—(happy are those who *never* do it)— she cannot be said to love with *all* the power of her heart.

To Gerald Mervyn she gave what Sydney had given to her, and in uniting her fate to his, she would voluntarily relinquish what had hitherto appeared essential to her very life of life. For, however much her husband might love her, Ellen never deceived herself by fancy- ing that it would be in the same measure that she *had* been loved—she would become the adorer rather than the adored.

But of this, and all the other risks connected with it, Ellen thought little, and cared less. She enjoyed a feverish, unwholesome sort of happiness, in anticipating the future, and grew mpatient when, the month of July being over,

Norah still made no arrangements for returning home.

This home, for both of them, was to be, at least for some little time, in Paris, and there Ellen had decided that *the meeting* should take place.

At length Norah perceived the restlessness of her companion, and as it had been for Ellen's pleasure even more than for her own that she had proposed the travelling, it cost her little to suggest the retracing of their steps.

So they went back, and took possession of a charming little apartment in the *quartier Beaujon*, that the young schoolmistress (before leaving Paris) had secured for them ; and where they both found letters from their respective friends waiting their arrival.

Ellen thus learned what she had been most anxious about—that her little girl was well and happy; then that Katherine was almost herself again, and that the whole family, including May, were going the next winter to London, where Mrs. Willand would meet them, being desirous of seeing and embracing her lost Sydney's daughter.

From St. Ives, Ellen received intelligence of the birth of a son to Maurice and his dear Gracie, and an earnest, affectionate entreaty, that she would soon come, with her child, and spend a long time amongst them.   They had none of them heard of her last illness until it was over, but they yearned inexpressibly to see her again, and appeared to think it a little odd that she should prefer the society of strangers.   Mrs. Clavering, finding the old cottage dull, after her long residence with the lively Mrs. Miniver, had consented to receive Miss Glossop—(left alone by her father's death)—as an inmate; and they got on exceedingly well together. "But we have plenty of space for you with us, dearest Nelly," wrote her brother—"and Gracie takes more delight in adorning the room that is to be yours than in supplying common necessaries to any other in the house. John is the only person who ever occupies it, and he comes very seldom, having a large flock to tend and keep in order. Come, pray come soon, or we shall be furiously jealous of this Miss Kennedy, who seems to have taken such entire possession of you."

Norah's letters were fewer and briefer, but one was of importance, inasmuch as it required her, if possible, to be in England within a week or fortnight at latest, from the time when she received it. The business was connected with the last poem she had published, and there seemed no choice but for her to obey the summons.

"But I cannot bear to leave you here alone," she said, as they were discussing the matter over a late tea. "Who knows what mischief you may get into during my absence?"

Ellen did not look quite so innocent as her friend expected her to do at this jesting remark, but she replied, laughingly also:—

"It must be a strange state of affairs which constitutes a single lady the watch-dog of her *chaperone*. What promise do you require from me?"

"None, except that you will not make your escape. I could ill afford to lose you now, Nelly."

"Well, so far I think you may trust me. But if you have still any doubts on the subject, what do you say to my taking this opportunity of paying Madame Jocelyn a visit? I am anxious to see how our young friend gets on with her new school."

" No, no—we will go together to Tours, for the winter, as we have promised. I can't trust you alone where teaching is going on, lest your romantic notions of independence should lead you into the commission of some folly that would deprive me of you altogether."

" Assuredly if it had not been for Mr. Wilmot's generosity, I should have proved to you that my feelings on the subject of independence extend beyond mere 'notions,' Norah. I am already sufficiently in debt to you, for a thousand things which money could never pay, without incurring pecuniary obligations as well. So when my present resources fail, depend on it I shall try whether all that fine education I received at Madame Guillemar's is worth anything."

" And what am *I* to do then ?"

"Oh, you must marry, Norah. With your money and good looks, and fame above all, you might have a tolerable choice of husbands if you pleased."

"Ah, but I don't please, my child; and if I did, the fame, as you call it, would be *against* me, and not *for* me in the matter. There is not one man in a thousand who can bear the idea of marrying a woman who writes. They have an idea that she must be pedantic, self-sufficient, and intensely disagreeable."

"I know one man who would not think so. Perhaps some day you may know him too."

Norah would not ask questions. Perhaps she had all along guessed that Ellen had a secret; but if so, she was patience and discretion personified, and having waited so long, she could easily restrain her curiosity a little longer.

Ellen received no encouragement to be communicative that night. And the next day Norah started for England.

CHAPTER XIV.

ELLEN did not write to Mr. Mervyn himself. She only said in a letter to Mr. Wilmot—" If you see Mr. Mervyn, be kind enough to let him know where I am."

And six days afterwards, Mr. Mervyn was in Paris.

Ellen had dwelt so often upon this meeting, had surrounded it in her imagination with so much romance and visible emotion; had been persuaded that, at least, the depth of her *own* feelings would betray themselves the moment she heard the sound of that voice concerning which she so frequently quoted to herself those lines from the most romantic poem in existence—

> " *Throughout the breathing world's extent,*
> *There was but one such voice for her,*
> *So kind, so soft, so eloquent."*

She had, I repeat, dwelt so often and so foolishly upon all this, that when Mr. Mervyn entered the room in which she was sitting, and shook hands with her as quietly and calmly as he had' used to do at the Glens, she was quite taken by surprise, and, except growing a little pale at the first moment, behaved very quietly and composedly herself.

Then he thanked her for complying with the request contained in his letter, and accepting her invitation to share her solitary meal (it was tea), began talking on general and indifferent subjects in his old manner, and without the slightest assumption that the former relations between them were in any degree changed.

In the end, poor Ellen grew nervous and alarmed. Could she have mistaken the purport of his letter altogether? Could she, during her long illness, have imagined the whole thing? Nonsense, he had already alluded to the letter; besides, was it not carefully locked away up-stairs amongst her most secret, cherished pos-sessions? and did she not know every word of it by heart? It was only that he was peculiar, and never did anything like common-place people. Presently he would speak out, and all would be clear between them.

Otherwise, what could she do with that vast heart-full of love, which was ready to be poured out upon him the instant he asked for it!

What, but hide it for ever, with herself, in

the cold grave, which would, in such a case, be her only refuge.

But Gerald Mervyn was not a cruel or a heartless man. He was quite as anxious as ever to add to the comfort and happiness of that young life which had been so early blighted; and which, in the absence of any other absorbing preoccupation, he had watched with such warm and genuine interest.

And at length, just before it was time to go, he told her all this, in his own rather brief but earnest and forcible language; and asked her whether she felt now, that a union with him would really and materially promote her happiness.

Then the woman's heart, with all its long-hoarded treasures of passionate and unreasoning devotion, of love, before which every obstacle is recklessly and triumphantly swept away, answered the appeal——And Gerald Mervyn was abundantly satisfied.

*   *   *   *   *

To Ellen it was the abrupt but radiant opening of a new life; the full entrance into a land of which she had scarcely had a glimpse, during her first short love dream, with him who afterwards became her husband.

Then she had always felt that her heart kept back a portion, the best portion, of its riches— *now* it gave all, and the life-long fever was assuaged.

With some natures, the craving *to be* loved is constant and insatiable, and, failing to obtain what they want, life is to them miserable and incomplete. Hitherto Ellen had fancied that hers was one of these natures; but present experience corrected this impression, and convinced her that to love, and not to *be loved,* was to her the only fullness of life, the only thing worth living for.

She was as completely lost, in the mazes of this bewildering passion, to all sense of that higher, spiritual existence, whose hopes and aims she was thus madly sacrificing, as David was up to the moment when the prophet came to him with those awful words,

"—Thou art the man!"

Alas! it seemed that she had passed under the rod, and heard its solemn and reproving voice so many times, *in vain.*

To those who have only a superficial knowledge of human nature, this total self abandonment on Ellen's part, might have appeared incomprehensible—for Gerald Mervyn was by no means an impassioned lover; and although he never by word, or look, or sign, did aught to make her question the *reality* of his attachment, it is equally true, that he gave very little outward expression to it. He was always kind, considerate, attentive, and even affectionate; but scarcely more so than he had been since the early days of their acquaintance in Scotland.

Had Ellen been less absorbed in her own wild love for him, she might have remarked this, and been uneasy about it ; but as it was, she remarked nothing that could in the least deteriorate from the intoxicating happiness she was enjoying.

When Mr. Mervyn had been about a week in Paris, Ellen wrote and told Norah everything, urging her to hasten home, that she might be introduced to him before his return to Scotland.

In her reply to this, Norah expressed no astonishment, but showed, against her will, that she was hurt by Ellen's long concealment of her attachment. She would be with them, however, the day after her letter was received, and in the meanwhile wished them joy from her very heart.

" Now, at least, you will tell me your friend's name," said Mr. Mervyn, to whom Ellen had been reading a part of Norah's letter—" I cannot at all enter into the spirit of the mystery."

" Never mind, Gerald," she said, laughing— " I must have my way in this little matter. I have told you that my friend is a famous authoress, and I want you, who know the works of every living writer, to guess when, you have seen and talked to her, which she is."

" As if I could ! when nearly all writers are, in fact, exactly the reverse of what their writings would lead you to imagine them ; besides, this lady, by your own acknowledgment, has so recently entered the field of literature, that the chances are I have never met with her works."

"Yes, you have; at any rate, in the reviews, which have, almost all, praised her extravagantly, and quoted largely from her writings. I wish I had been an authoress, Gerald."

"Why?"

"For your sake. You would have been so proud of me."

"Too proud, perhaps. Be content, Nelly— Don't you know what one of the sisterhood herself says on the subject?"

"No."

"This—

> *Happy, happier far than thou,*
> *With the laurel on thy brow,*
> *She that makes the humblest hearth*
> *Lovely but to one on earth."*

The tears came into Ellen's eyes.

"Ah yes; after all, I shall not envy Mrs. Hemans herself, if I can only make *you* happy, Gerald."

He took her hand, smiling a little at her enthusiasm, and said she might be quite sure that she would do *that*.

Everything seemed going on very smoothly between them. They had not even had one legitimate lover's quarrel yet.

*   *   *   *   *   •

Norah arrived in the morning, so that the friends were sure of a long day together before there would be any interruption to their *tête-à-tête*. As yet they had made no acquaintances in Paris, and Mr. Mervyn had business f his own to transact, which would prevent his joining them before the evening.

So Norah had once more to play the part of listener—an easy one to her always—and to be persuaded that this time Nelly had made no mistake, that he who would henceforth preside over her destiny was, in truth, *the one* in the whole world created for her, and who must inevitably fill her life with a happiness she had only dreamt of till now.

"Say you like him, Norah," she pleaded, childishly; "that you retract all the injurious suspicions you had once formed of him ; that you justify me a little, at any rate, in the love I have for him."

"My dear Nelly, you are far too impatient and unreasonable. I am quite prepared to like your friend, for I think I see much that is really estimable and worthy in his character; but I shall be in a position to tell you more about it at eleven o'clock to-night—he won't stay longer than that, will he ?"

"Oh, Norah, I never thought you cold or cynical till now—now, when your kindness and sympathy would have been so precious to me."

"Don't let us quarrel, Nelly. I am very far from meaning to be unkind to you. It is not my fault if my nature is more inclined to sympathize with sorrow than with joy—besides, you forget that you are requiring me to sing songs of gladness, in the prospect of losing something that had become the sunshine of my dull, grey life."

"Forgive me, dear, dear Norah, and love me still," exclaimed Ellen, full of contrition for what she had said, and, indeed, vexed with herself altogether; "my happiness has not made me amiable, whatever else it has done. Let us talk of other things, and put this odious and obtrusive self of mine aside for a little."

"Till this evening, when it *must* come forth again, and sit enthroned in its fullness of joy. Who knows but what, in my heart, I envy you, Nelly?"

"Poor Norah!"

"Don't say that again, Nelly. I can bear pity least of all things. And assuredly it is not your Mr. Mervyn whom I envy you."

"Ah, wait till you know him."

"I am waiting."

CHAPTER XV.

THEY had gone to watch the sunset, and to enjoy the freshening air in the pleasant shady garden, which they shared in common with ˙ the other inmates of the large house where they had made their home.

Mr. Mervyn was very late, and Ellen had begun to imagine all sorts of things, while Norah only thought his tardiness said little for his anxiety to form the acquaintance of his friend's friend.

At last came a ring at the outer gate, and

Ellen bidding Norah follow quickly, darted away to meet the new arrival, and to accompany him into the house.

"I thought you would never come, Gerald. I feared something had happened. What has kept you so long?"

"Nothing very important, dear; but I knew you would have a companion, so I did not hurry."

"As if *any* companion could atone to me for not having you!"

"My love, you will make me vain," he said; smiling, and stroking the little white hand, very thin still, which she had placed in his; "but where is this celebrity, this mysterious, nameless lady, now? Is she to be introduced to me with a door or a screen between us? Upon my word, I am growing curious about her, in spite of myself. If you do not bring her forth presently, I shall be sure that she is nothing but a myth, after all."

"I left her in the garden. She will be here in a minute; and now, while I have time, just let me caution you, Gerald, not to think her cold or ungracious, however she may behave to you at first. Occasionally, her manners are odd, but her heart is always right, and warm and true."

Norah might have heard these last words, for she was at the door when Ellen spoke them. She came in very composedly, and with the quietest smile upon her lips, as if, while she meant to receive her friend's lover in a friendly spirit, she would not have him suppose she had any very rapturous welcome to give him, *as* that lover.

He was standing between the two windows with his back to the light, Ellen close beside him, with her face upturned, (for he was a tall man), and her whole attitude strangely expressive of the deep, deep reverence and love she felt for him.

So Norah thought, in the brief glance she had of them both, on entering the room.

The next moment Ellen had moved forward, and was saying in her pleasantest voice, broken only by a little girlish inclination to laugh at the unravelling of the grand mystery—

" Miss Norah Kennedy, and Mr. Gerald Mervyn, let me introduce you. I foresee that you will be such good friends by and bye, that I need not expatiate to either on the merits of the other. Come, Gerald, let us hear what pretty speech you have prepared to greet the lady ' with the laurel on her brow.' "

But Gerald, notwithstanding this playful adjuration, neither spoke nor moved ; and when

Ellen turned in surprise to look at him, she saw that he was gazing, with an intentness, that deepened every moment, into the face of the lady standing midway between him and the still open door.

" What's the matter ?"

Whether she spoke these words, or only thought them, Ellen never knew. In another instant, her whole observation was directed to Norah, who, white as a corpse, and with lips that trembled visibly, seemed on the point of. enacting some tragic and alarming scene.

If this had gone on, poor Ellen would undoubtedly have cried aloud, and implored her two companions to end for her the cruel, agonising suspense in which their behaviour placed her ; but on a sudden, as if by the influence of some hidden magic power, Norah recovered herself, and, advancing with outstretched hand to Mr. Mervyn, thus addressed him :—

"In spite of the change of name, which I was unprepared for, I believe I recognize an old friend, to whom I scarcely need an introduction. At first you seemed so like an apparition from the dead, that I was positively frightened as well as bewildered. Nelly must excuse us both. It is such long, long years since we have met."

"And now to meet in this way! Norah Kennedy—little Norah Kennedy, my old play-fellow!"

It was all he said, as holding both her hands, he still stood looking eagerly into her now admirably disciplined face, and trying to trace therein some likeness to the plain but intelligent features he so well remembered.

But Ellen?

Well, she too had, happily, a certain power of concealing her strongest emotions, when any urgent necessity existed for so doing. Con-

sequently, after a few minutes of doubt and perplexity, she went quietly to the tea-table, and
began making the tea.

The others continued talking and recurring
to old times, as if they were alone together; or
as if the third party in the room must necessarily
feel the same interest and delight in these re-
miniscences that they did themselves.

She listened very attentively at any rate,
listened with every faculty fully awakened, with
every nerve of mental sensation strained to that
degree of tightness when each breath that passes
over them, however soft, becomes burning pain.

" I was told that you were married, years
ago," she heard Gerald say, and Norah replied
that she could not imagine how such a report
had arisen, since, in all her life, there had never
been the slightest question of such a thing.

" And you are an authoress!—I am not surprised. Those crude, strange fancies that you used to have as a child; that dream-land in which you used to live; those woman-thoughts before their time—all this could have but one result, unless you had fulfilled the commoner destiny of your sex, and suffered a human love to engulf both your genius and its requirements."

" I was wiser, you see—" (She tried to speak gaily, but succeeded ill.)

He was about to reply, when Ellen, in rather a quickened, but otherwise perfectly unsuggestive voice, asked them if they would not come and have some tea— it would be cold else.

Then they both thought of her, and came to the table.

Of course nothing else *could be* spoken of but the strangeness of this accidental meeting— after so many years—under such remarkable circumstances ! Mr. Mervyn spoke of it, Norah spoke of it, Ellen spoke of it; and though they all tried, when the tea-things had been removed, to get upon more general topics of conversation, it would not do. That which was uppermost in the mind and heart of each, could not be superseded by subjects of only ordinary interest; and as Ellen, when once she had expressed all the astonishment and wonder that the case demanded, in the most approved conventional terms—had really nothing else to say about the matter, it was natural, if not inevitable, that the *two* should, in the end, have all the conversation to themselves, and that she, appearing to be intently occupied with some work she had taken up, should once more be entirely forgotten.

For the first time since Ellen had known Mr. Mervyn, he shone to-night with his fullest lustre—as a man of rare talent, refined intellect, andε ntensely poetical, rather than passionately human, feeling. He had met a really kindred spirit—one who could thoroughly understand him, and whom he could thoroughly understand.

Poor Ellen had only loved him with all the powers of her loving heart. Till now she had fancied that he was satisfied with this.

Till now !

Oh, would the evening never end? Had Time indeed stood still, like Joshua's moon in Ajalon, for the purpose of lengthening out a torture of which one minute's duration might have contented the vengeance of her bitterest foe? Or was there some mocking demon present, distorting all things to her mental view?

It seemed like it—for they—the two by the window, where the rays from Ellen's lamp scarcely fell, could not believe, when the clock struck eleven, that it was half so late They

were sure the hands must have been mis-
chievously put on.   And when it was discovered
that the watches told the same tale, Mr. Mervyn
laughingly declared, that Time itself had entered
into a wicked conspiracy against them.

The quiet worker thought so too, only it was
the other way.

But at length he rose to bid the ladies good-
night, and to ask Ellen, (which he did in his
kindest voice), to pardon his apparent neglect
for this once, he really could not help it; but it
should never happen again.

He was far too preoccupied to notice the
"pale trouble" in the face she lifted for a moment to his, in giving him her hand, and wishing
him good-night.

How the others parted, matters not.   They
had had time enough to become alive to their
actual position now.

Norah went up and kissed Ellen, with more than even her usual fondness, the instant they were alone. If Ellen recoiled, it was so slightly that her friend did not perceive it.

" We have been very rude, and very selfish, haven't we, dear Nelly ? you have a great deal to forgive : but you are generous, and *will* forgive us, I know. The surprise was so great, you can fancy that. I have not yet half recovered from it."

This was plain enough. She was looking more excited, and nearly as white as Ellen herself, who made some general remark about the pleasure of meeting old friends, and her own entire disposition to sympathize with this pleasure.

Norah seemed wanting to say something else, but as if she did not know exactly in what words to put it.

At length, as Ellen took up a bed-room can-dle, and by a succession of yawns intimated that she was dying to get to bed, Norah again approached her caressingly.

"Dearest Nelly, I must just say, before we part for the night, that you are not for one moment to think that the happiness I have felt in meeting Gerald Mervyn again, is less-ened by the fact of meeting him as *your* future husband. It is increased by it, you may believe it."

Then, without waiting for Ellen's answer, without even looking into her face, she went out of the room.

And Ellen went to bed.

CHAPTER XVI.

I BELIEVE that in most human lives, perhaps in all that extend beyond the boundary of childhood, there occurs a season, more or less prolonged, in which the heart suffers not only to the utmost limit of its capacity for suffering, but exactly that definite *kind* of pain in its fullest measure, to which that particular heart is most acutely susceptible.

I believe, moreover, that until that hour arrives, no living being knows, or can know the *kind* of weapon that has the keenest and most deadly power to wound him.

This season—this inevitable season—(supposing my theory correct), had arrived to-night for Ellen Willand.

Suffering was not new to her. She had experienced it already under various aspects, chiefly when her young husband's sudden death took from her life a gladness and a brightness to which she had grown lovingly familiar, and afterwards, when the sense of desolation and loneliness grew into a dull, constant pain, that was like a cold mist overhanging a once fair and sunny prospect. All this was suffering, genuine and unquestionable suffering, that must leave traces of its footsteps upon the heart and in the life.

But it bore no resemblance at all to the sufferings of the present night.

They were not of a nature to be talked about, or analyzed, for the gratification of the curious. They had no order in them, nothing to make them worthy of record amongst those subtle and unexplainable emotions of the human mind, which clever men sometimes love to dissect and classify, in the same manner that geologists deal with their fossils and stones.

The sufferings to which I am alluding were simple and common enough, I daresay, (alas! that sin should have left such a necessity in our unhappy world!) but to the poor heart they now visited, they were new and strange, and appalling.

Ellen's was not a strong or vigorous nature—I have said so before—and she had never believed herself capable of anything like the fierce throbs of agony that came and went in her swelling and fevered veins to-night. She had learnt, on former occasions, how anxiety, how bereavement, how utter loneliness, moral and actual, could affect her.

But it was reserved for this special hour to teach her what jealousy could do.

" Strong as death, cruel as the grave; the coals thereof are coals of fire, which hath a most vehement flame."

So she felt it.

And outwardly, throughout all, she was perfectly calm and composed.   Lying in bed, and with wide-open eyes fixed on the white drapery of the muslin curtains, not a muscle of her face changing, not the slightest restlessness of the body giving token of the mind's raging and impetuous fever—who could have suspected that anything unusual was the matter?

For who could know what those wide-open eyes were seeing all the time?

Oh, mother earth! take thy children to thy quiet bosom, and spare them such sights as those; spare them the draining of that cup of deadly bitterness, which, whatever their after-lives may be, *must* leave something of its soul-revolting taste behind.

Half the night had gone by before Ellen's mind took in anything beyond acute sensation, and that of a purely personal kind; but at length a distinct purpose was suggested to it, admitted, and finally resolved on.

After this, she arose and began walking about her room, watching eagerly for the dawn to appear; looking, as she had never looked before, at the starlit, purple sky; and wondering, as she had used to wonder as a little child, whether the Great God really dwelt in some bright and glorious local habitation above that canopy of clouds.

If He did, whether He saw and compassion-
ated her present misery, and would do anything
to relieve or mitigate it.

To His children He said indeed, " Cast thy
burden upon me, and I will sustain thee."
But what did He say to the rebellious and dis-
obedient, to those who, having been often re-
proved, had only hardened their necks, and gone
on frowardly in the way of their own hearts?

Alas! she did not know. But she knelt
down, and tried, in her anguish, to pray.   •

No sensible relief came now. The feelings
were all too restless and excited for that; the
heart and brain were in too fierce a tumult for
the dove of peace to enter in; but something
came, notwithstanding, while she was upon her
knees.

It was the sudden, strong, changeless conviction that this was the punishment of her

sin, in forgetting God, and making to herself an idol of clay. It was a voice that spoke to her inmost soul, and said—" Thy sin hath found thee out !" " The rod is for the backs of fools." " Hast thou not procured this unto thyself, in that thou hast forsaken the Lord thy God, when He led thee by the way ?"

Yes, so far it was quite and for ever clear to her; and had the one great misery been less, Ellen would have experienced much alarm and agitation at the thought of being under God's anger, and thus alienated from Him, as a child is alienated from a parent whose love and kindness it has exhausted. Even as it was, old habits of thought sufficiently prevailed, to fill her with a sort of awe at the position in which she believed herself to be—measuring the magnitude of her sin by the magnitude of its punishment.

(And here I must just state that I am only giving the thoughts and impressions of a poor, tortured soul, under the sudden influence of the most passionate sorrow it had ever known. I am not setting dówn, either suggestively or didactically, any opinions of my own on the solemn subject of God's dealings with His creatures in the matter of temporal punishment for sin.)

But the present moment was not one in which any thoughts connected with spiritual things were likely to prevail. No human passion, not even love itself, is so entirely absorbing while it lasts, or has such resistless power to sweep down all before it, as jealousy—" the worm that will not sleep, and never dies."

In Ellen's case it was accompanied with one, I believe, peculiar feature ; she felt no anger, not the very slightest, towards either Gerald or Norah. Their injury to her had been so unconscious, so unpremeditated. One of the sights that she had seen oftenest, during those long, wakeful hours, was Norah sitting on the floor in her little bedroom at school, with the old, yellow letters beside her. Ellen had good reason to know how true and strong that early love had been, how constant, how enduring! It ought to find its reward.

Surely it *had* done so.

There was no mistaking Gerald's fervent admiration; his almost passionate delight in finding his old playfellow again, and finding her transformed into a highly intellectual, fascinating woman, who had already mounted many steps of that pedestal of fame which he himself would have been well content to have ascended —which now, perhaps, he *would* ascend, having such a companion to urge him on.

Not that Ellen for a moment imagined that

either of them had an idea of behaving what the
world would call " ill to her."   Norah's was just
the character to glory in the loftiest self-sacri-
fice ; besides, Ellen was quite aware how very
dear she herself was to this friend of old days,
and that loving her as Norah did, the resignation
of her own happiness would be to her comparatively easy.   Gerald Mervyn, too, with his kind
heart, and strictly honourable feeling, would
never dream of the possibility of dissolving that
engagement which he had appeared so anxious .
to contract; of destroying for ever the happiness he had so earnestly desired to promote.

Oh no, Ellen did them both full justice ; but
her course was none the less clear on this
account.   The pangs of that night had been
too bitter and too deadly, to give her any wish
of procuring them for herself for a life-time.

Besides, a voice had spoken to her—it had told her that the idol *must* be given up, and her very weakness and timidity enabled her to obey.

She had collected what she could of her clothes together, and huddled them anyhow into a box, as soon as the light appeared. She intended getting away by stealth, and leaving a letter for Norah explaining all; but just as she had taken out writing materials, and, with her bonnet on, was sitting down to write, the door of her room opened noiselessly, (she had forgotten to lock it,) and Norah herself stood before her, looking in amazement at the littered apartment, and at Ellen's costume.

"Why, Nelly, what is all this? you have given me quite a turn."

Perhaps she meant thus to account for her own pale cheeks, and the other indications of a sleepless, agitated night, that her appearance presented.

Ellen grew very red for a moment, then, rising from her table, she went up to Norah and took her hand.

"I am sorry you came in. It would have been better for both of us had I written as I intended. We are neither of us in a condition for talking much this morning, indeed my head is rather confused. You too look dreadfully ill, dear Norah. Kiss me, and go back to bed,· there's a good child."

" And you, Nelly ?"

" I am going to Tours, that is all."

" Then I will go with you, so that is soon settled."

" No, you must not. Indeed I would rather go alone."

" Nelly, my dear, dear Nelly," (she wound

her arms tightly round the poor girl, whose physical strength was fast giving way,) " did you believe what I said to you last night? or do you think that the friendship I have so long professed for you, has been all a sham, a delusion ? Speak, my child, say something to comfort me. I am very unhappy—for you, Nelly."

" Norah," the other said, in a solemn though quivering voice—" God is my witness that I do you and your generous friendship ample justice. I never, never could repay one half of what I owe you. Hereafter, if we both live, we shall meet again and be happy ; but let me go now, in pity let me go. I will write more."

" One other question, Nelly, and I have done. Do you doubt Gerald's love for you ?"

The blood retreated from Ellen's face, and gathered round her heart, which began to beat violently ; but she said slowly and distinctly —

" Norah, I know now. I have known since last night that his affection for me, born of pity, has never reached the passion of love at all. My own infatuation blinded me to this fact before, though it ought not to have done so, having had my poor Sydney's love to compare with Mr. Mervyn's. I have been in a dream ; but now I am thoroughly awake. You can explain all."

" I think not ; besides, if you persist in going to Tours, I shall accompany you."

" Then I will go somewhere else—to England, if you like—anywhere."

" At least, see Gerald once before you go. You owe him this, Nelly."

" I dare not—" then repenting these words —" I mean that it would only be prolonging pain to us all. Norah, hear me. Come what may, whether you, who ought to be his wife, marry him or not, I swear most solemnly that I will never do so. God has heard the vow. Now will you let me go quietly?"

Norah looked unspeakably distressed. She sat down and covered her face with her hands for several minutes. At length her perplexity was over.

"Nelly, will you go to England, and send for your little girl, and then take her with you to your friends in the north? You would be happy with your mother and brother."

"I would much rather, for the present, go and work hard amongst strangers."

"And break your heart, as well as ours. Nelly, do as I ask you. You say you owe me something—discharge the debt by this little sacrifice."

"And if I do, you will remain here?"

"Only till I can give up our apartment and

make preparations for going elsewhere. Don't think, Nelly, that I, who have loved you as one woman rarely loves another, could build my happiness upon the ruin of yours. As far as *I* am concerned, your heroism will be more than wasted."

" It is not heroism, Norah."

" Well, call it what you please. And now you had better sit down, and write to Gerald. I shall not see him."

Ellen had been partly prepared for all this, . though, by going away, she had hoped to escape it for awhile; but to argue with or resist a nature so much stronger than her own, was not her habit, except in the very extremest cases.

So when Norah left her, she once more took up a pen, and, in a few calm and friendly words, signed away the happiness of her life.

This is often done, sometimes through the influence, or by the compulsion of others, sometimes because conscience imperatively demands it; and sometimes, as in Ellen's case, because circumstances have left the sufferer nothing else to do.   And the receivers of such letters perhaps rarely guess that the poor heart has opened and bled with every word, expressing less than passionate agony, that the hand has traced.

In an hour from the time Ellen had sealed and addressed her last words to Gerald Mervyn, she was on her way to England.

.

CHAPTER XVII.

NORAH KENNEDY TO GERALD MERVYN.

" IN enclosing to you, as I faithfully promised to do, the accompanying letter, I have
only a few words to say on my own account.
They are these.

" I have known Ellen Willand since we were
girls at school together—loved her dearly all the
time. Her present conduct has grieved and
surprised me more than I can easily express.   I
have done all in my power to dissuade her from
it, but have not succeeded.   She questions the

depth of your love for her, and believes that she
is only sacrificing *herself* in releasing you from
your engagement.   If this *is* the case, I counsel
you to accept the freedom she offers—Ellen will
recover her peace of mind, and be happy again
one of these days, with her child and the friends
who warmly love and cherish her, as she deserves to be loved and cherished.   She would
be miserable as your wife, did you give her the
slightest ground to suspect that your whole
heart was not devoted to her.

"But if, on the other hand, you do *really*
love her, so as to make this dissolution of your
engagement a source of unhappiness to you too,
then I counsel you strongly to go after her, and,
in spite of vows and protestations, win her back
to you again.   She has a gentle, clinging, tenderly loving nature, and would soon be persuaded of her present error—if an error it be.

"Anyhow, forgive me if I decline to meet you again at present. I have been strangely upset by Ellen's abrupt departure, and the circumstances attending it.

"Your happiness is my fervent prayer.

"NORAH KENNEDY."

GERALD MERVYN TO NORAH KENNEDY.

"I thank you sincerely for what you have written, although your letter, no less than that of your friend, has filled me with perplexity and distress. Before they came, I had looked down closely into the depths of my own heart, and seen that Ellen did *not* hold there the place that my wife *should* hold. I knew her in her sorrow and desolation, Norah—pitied her, liked her, admired her to a certain extent, and felt, when she was free, that there would be a satisfaction worth obtaining, in atoning to her for the trials of the past. From the time of our engagement, I have feared that the love was unequal—I have hated myself for it, for indeed, as you say, she is a gentle, trusting woman, and worthy of being loved—but these things are beyond our control. I felt so last night, when I met again the little girl who had once filled all my boyish heart, and who would have been my wife (for surely you loved me then, Norah) had not a mother, whose will I never disputed, interposed and changed my destiny.

" But to return to Ellen—I am cut to the heart in thinking that she is suffering, and suffering through me, who had so prided myself on making her happy. If by following her, I could restore things to their original footing, I would do it gladly, in spite of——no, I will not say that *yet*—but you know, Norah, this would be impossible—she saw too clearly—poor tender, sensitive heart! Besides, she has taken a vow never to be my wife. Better, therefore, let the matter rest as it is—you have said so.

"But in the meanwhile, I implore you to grant me one interview—we will only speak of her; I promise it you—and to-morrow I shall return to Scotland.

"Yours, in ancient friendship,

"GERALD."

NORAH KENNEDY TO GERALD MERVYN.

"No, Gerald—I have decided wisely, I am sure, in refusing to see you now. I am going to an old friend at Tours, for the present. There I shall hear from Ellen, and from thence I will write to you. God bless you.

"NORAH.

"P.S. Ellen will want her child brought to

her from Scotland. Could you not perform this little service for her ?"

Two months later, Norah received at Tours, where she was staying with Madame Jocelyn, the following letter from Ellen Willand.

"My Dearest Norah,

"I told you, in the few lines that announced my safe arrival in England, that I should not write again till I felt better in mind and body. Truly it was a sore sickness—soul sickness—that oppressed me then; but its violence is mitigated; its exceeding bitterness, God be praised, is passing away. While waiting for my little girl from Scotland, I have been staying with Mrs. Lane—she knows all my history, and she has helped me, by her sympathy and prayers, to support my burden quietly, if not bravely. Indeed I am much better, Norah, and May is a great comfort to me. You know who brought her to me, for it was you who suggested it. Dear Norah, I wonder what your motive was. However, the meeting did me no harm—rather the reverse, I think—he was so kind, so very kind and considerate, in every way; and I—well, I believe I was tolerably composed—but it seemed strange, at first, to look at him, and think of him as *not my own*, as no more to me than the veriest stranger. I am positive it would help me a great deal in forgetting him if I were sure, quite sure that he was going to be your husband. You would suit each other so well, and I could pray for you both *together*—that you might learn (what I hope my life's discipline has taught *me*) to seek your best happiness above this present world, not to trust in *it alone*, for anything!

" I am waiting in London now for the family from the Glens. Katherine wishes to have May with her for a few days, before I take her into the country; and next year, all being well, we are both, May and myself, to go and spend some months with them in Scotland. So it seems they have forgiven me for leaving them as I did. I wish, Norah, I might find you, (not exactly at the Glens), but *near* it, when I go. It would make me happy, indeed it would.

" I have been to see Gertrude Lomond once since I came to England. She has now four children, of whom two are twins, and is as busy and happy as a bee amongst them. A strange ending for the blue stocking, is it not? stitch, stitch, stitch, from morning till night, and books of all kinds a totally prohibited luxury.

" Write me a full account of yourself, dear Norah, of Miss Jane, (I cannot call her anything else), and of the young governess of the Avenue Marbœuf. Above all, tell me that you will no longer suffer a ridiculous shadow to stand between you and the sun, which ought to have shone upon you years and years ago. *He* told me all about it.

"Yours ever, in fond affection,

"NELLY."

CHAPTER XVIII.

It had once done Ellen good to watch the current of John Arnold's life; a life of quiet, unostentatious usefulness, flowing on in the appointed course of duty, and never pausing to seek for itself what the world calls happiness; this had done her good, by rebuking that spirit of selfish ease, in which, at that time, she had so many temptations to indulge; but it did her . more good now, because her mind was in a better and more plastic state, from the furnace heat which had passed over it, to watch the daily lives of her brother and his humble, Christian wife.

It was to them she came, with her little daughter, a few weeks after the period of her last letter to Norah Kennedy.

Nothing could present a stronger contrast to the life Ellen herself had led, than the simple lives she had now to contemplate. At first they had seemed to her strangely devoid of interest, dull, monotonous, common-place, filled up with trivialities that sometimes wearied her, and sometimes made her feel almost angry when she saw that they were dignified by the serious notice of those around her; how could they stoop to care about, or even talk about, such *little* things?

But, by degrees, this wore off; the small village-life amalgamated with her own, in some degree, once more. The petty hopes and fears, the comparatively trifling interests, the quarrels and reconciliations of even this "little people," (necessarily narrow - minded and ignorant,) ceased to appear so contemptible as in the beginning they had done. The human element, bearing about everywhere its electric chain, *must* strike some fire, happily, into all who come within its circle.

And then Maurice and his wife, though they possessed far simpler minds than Ellen had recently been familiar with, read few books besides their Bible, and those of a strictly religious character, and cared for nothing that had not in it *some* elements of spirituality, were both of them so genuinely cheerful, so unmistakably happy in their home, their duties, their child and each other, that it was impossible, in living with them, not to admire, love, and wish to imitate.

If a fault could be found, it was in their constant and untiring petting of Ellen and her blue-eyed image, and their determination to persist in this course, even at the risk of making them both the very reverse of what they wished them to be.

Perhaps they thought that Ellen had suffered enough, or that, if more discipline were needed, it would be sure to come in its appointed time. While she was resting by the palm-trees, there could be no sin or danger in trying to make that rest as sweet as it might be to her.

She had been two months at St. Ives before she saw John Arnold.

Then he came and stayed a week with them, and it was a happy time for all; for him especially.

The winter, invariably long and severe in the

north, was unmarked by any event of importance, except the temporary illness of Mrs.
Clavering, during which Ellen went to nurse
her mother, and won, by her patience and gentleness, (skill was not admitted,) the favourable
opinion of her old directress, Miss Glossop,
who told her, in confidence, that if she (Ellen)
had not been unfortunate enough to get
amongst the dissenters, she might have been
made something of after all.

The spring passed rapidly, only too rapidly
they all said; for, in the month of June, Ellen
was to take May to London, and from thence
proceed with the Wilmots on a long visit to
Scotland. Very recently, she had been led to
indulge a hope—it was indeed a hope now—
that she should find a friend there, whom she
longed ardently to see again.

It was about a week before the time fixed for

her departure, when one evening, Maurice and Gracie both being out, a letter was delivered to her from Norah. She took it into the little arbour in the garden, and there, screened from all observation, read it once, twice, thrice, while her tears fell like rain upon the unconscious paper.

They were not unhappy tears, but they came very fast for all that, and a stranger, looking in suddenly upon her, might have supposed her afflicted with some violent grief.

Before the shadows fell, a stranger did look in upn her — somebody, at least, whose advent was wholly unexpected, and whose abrupt appearance there caused her to utter an exclamation of startled astonishment.

It was John Arnold.

"I hope I have not frightened you, Ellen," he said, advancing to where she sat, and shaking hands, " but I found nobody in the house, and so came here."

" No, they are all out, Maurice and Gracie over the common, visiting some of their sick, and May spending the day with grandmamma. But what a surprise to see you here—we had no idea you were coming."

" I heard that you were leaving in a week, and I wanted to see you before you went; so I have stolen a holiday."

" It is very kind of you. I am delighted that you are come."

But she spoke rather absently, and he soon saw that she had been crying.

" What has happened, Ellen?—Have you had any bad news?—I see a letter beside you."

" No, I have had very good news. A dear friend—the friend, indeed, with whom I was so long abroad after my illness, is just married, happily married, and—and I am glad."

" And therefore you cry?"

"I am very foolish, but there are associations connected with this event which—I mean thinking of them just now, have agitated me a good deal. I would tell you more about them; but it is a long story, and would weary you. Won't you come into the house, and let me make you some tea?"

"No, thank you. Do you remember, Ellen, the first time you ever made tea for me—long, long ago? at least it seems so now. Poor girl! you have suffered a little since then."

" Yes."

"Ellen, I want to speak to you. Are you composed enough to listen to me to-night?"

" Certainly "

" Well, then, I want to ask you when you

come back from Scotland to share my home, to be my dear wife, and to let me love you openly, as I have long done in secret, as it has become pain to do in secret, and as I shall glory in doing before the world."

It was a long time before she answered him at all, and though he tried in every way, it was too dark for him to see her face distinctly. At length she said—

" I am not worthy to be your wife. This I feel from the very depths of my heart. But listen now to the story I feared to weary you by telling you just now."

He listened.•

When it was done—nothing concealed, nothing palliated,—she said very humbly and sorrowfully—

" Your wife should not come to you with a heart all torn and bruised as mine has been.

You deserve something far better than this."

"Ellen, answer me one question. Do you believe that eternal wisdom has led *you* wisely, has appointed you exactly the trials best qualified for disciplining and sanctifying your nature? can you, from your heart, say of all the past, ' it is well?' "

"Yes—I have not the shadow of a doubt on the subject."

"Then how can I, an erring mortal myself, complain or regret? God has permitted me to love you—He only knows how well—and through whatever paths He may have led you, I am satisfied since He has led you to Himself, and—I hope to *me*. Now, Ellen, tell me if *you* are content, and if you will try to love me, and trust me with your earthly happiness."

" I will try to be deserving of your love," she said. " For the rest, I have not much need to try."

He took her for a moment to his heart, and felt, for the first time in his life, that earth might bear some flowers of a lost paradise even for him.

In the quiet of her own room that night, Ellen wrote to Norah a long, long letter, breathing of peace and full contentment in every line.

Thus it ended.

" And so you see, dear Norah, after all, you have married the man of intellect, the man of refinement—the ideal of our youthful dreams ! And I am going to marry—*Only a good man !*"

Her heart was full ; and sinking on her

knees, by a sudden and uncontrollable impulse, she murmured, with tears of fervent and passionate gratitude—

"Father, I thank Thee that this good man is mine."

THE END.

BILLING, PRINTER AND STEREOTYPER, GUILDFORD, SURREY.

III.

Mr. W. A. Ross's New Work.

In 2 vols. post 8vo. price 21s.

AN OLD ROAD AND AN OLD RIVER.

By WILLIAM A. Ross,

Author of "A Yacht Voyage to Norway, Sweden, and Denmark,"
&c. &c.

IV.

Mr. Platt's New Novel.

In 3 vols., price 31s. 6d.

THE STORY OF A LOST LIFE.

By WILLIAM PLATT,

Author of "Betty Westminster," "Mothers and Sons," &c.

V.

In 2 vols., price 21s.

THE ONE TRIAL.

VI.

In 1 vol. post 8vo., price 10s. 6d.

THE PERILS OF ENGLAND;

or, Volunteers and Invasions, in 1796-7-8—1805, and at the
Present Time.

By HUMPHREY BLUNT.

VII.

In 1 vol., price 10s. 6d.

MY VILLAGE NEIGHBOURS.

By Miss STERNE.

" Miss Sterne writes agreeably and with facility, after the fashion
of Miss Mitford."—*Athenæum.*

" There is great power in these volumes. The author possesses
a very unusual command of language, and a rare degree of pathos."
—*Morning Herald.*

" The style is rustic and simple, and thoroughly entertaining."—
Court Journal.

" We have read nothing equal to it since the publication of
Miss Mitford's ' Our Village.' "—*Scottish Press.*

" Miss Sterne deserves every credit for having written a very
pleasant book."—*Morning Post.*

MR. NEWBY'S NEW PUBLICATIONS.

NEW NOVELS.

I.
In 1 vol. post 8vo., price 10s. 6d.

ADAM BEDE, JUNIOR.
A SEQUEL.

II.
In 2 vols. post 8vo. price 21s.

COMING EVENTS CAST THEIR SHADOWS BEFORE.

III.
In 1 vol., price 10s. 6d.

MY COUNTRY NEIGHBOURS.
By G. M. STERNE,
Great-Cousin of Laurence Sterne, author of the "Sentimental Journey."

IV.
In 3 vols. post 8vo., price 31s. 6d. (In November.)

THE GREAT EXPERIMENT.
By MISS MOLESWORTH,
Author of the "Stumble on the Threshold," &c.

V.
In 1 vol. fcap. 8vo., price 4s. (Now ready.)

GLAD TIDINGS.

VI.
In 3 vols. post 8vo., price 31s. 6d. (In December.)

TRIED IN THE FIRE.
By MRS. MACKENZIE DANIELS,
Author of "My Sister Minnie," "The Old Maid of the Family," &c.

VII.

In 3 vols. post. 8vo., price 31s. 6d.   (In November.)

THE HOME AND THE PRIEST.

By SIGNOR VOLPE,

Author of "Memoirs of an Ex-Capuchin; or Scenes in Monastic Life in Italy."

The late Leigh Hunt's opinion of the work :—"I think the work interesting; its exhibitions, in particular of some of the passions, masterly; and I am also of opinion that all which is related of Italian manners and customs, and of the vices and machinations of the priesthood, would be extremely welcome to my countrymen in general."

VIII.

In 3 vols., price 31s. 6d.

THE FATE OF FOLLY.

By LORD B********,

Author of "Masters and Workmen," &c.

"This is one of the very few works of fiction that should be added to every Public Free Library. It contains more moral lessons, more to elevate the minds of readers, and has higher aims than almost any novel we have read. At the same time, it is replete with incident and amusement."—*Globe.*

"It is a good book."—*Spectator.*

IX.

In 3 vols., price 31s. 6d.

BETTY WESTMINSTER.

By W. PLATT, Esq.

"A lesson of sound practical morality, inculcated with charming effect;—a story which bears in every chapter the impress of intellect, taste, and sensibility."—*Morning Post.*

"Betty Westminster is the representative of a type of society but little used by novelists—the money-getting tradesmen of provincial towns. It is written with talent and considerable skill."—*New Quarterly Review.*

"There is a great deal of cleverness in this story."—*Examiner.*

"There is much comic satire in it. The author has power worth cultivating."—*Examiner.*

"There is a good deal of spirit in these volumes, and great talent shown in the book."—*Athenæum.*

"A book of greater interest has not come under our notice for years."—*Review.*

"All is described by a master hand."—*John Bull*

X.

In 3 vols., price 31s. 6d.

GEORGIE BARRINGTON.

By the Author of "Old Memories," &c.

" This novel is full of power, full of interest, and full of those fascinations and spells which none but the extraordinarily-gifted can produce."—*Globe.*

XI.

In 2 vols. post 8vo., price 21s.

BEVERLEY PRIORY.

" This is an admirable tale."—*Naval and Military.*
" Beverley Priory is in no part of it a dull novel, and is unquestionably clever."—*Examiner.*

XII.

In 3 vols., price 31s. 6d.

THE PARSON AND THE POOR.

" There is much that is very good in this tale; it is cleverly written, and with good feeling."—*Athenæum.*
" We have read this novel with a great deal of pleasure; the dialogue is always spirited and natural. The children talk like children, and the men and women remind us of flesh and blood."—*Morning Herald.*
" The characters and incidents are such as will live in the memory of the reader, while the style and spirit of the book will render it not only pleasant but profitable reading."—*Bradford Review.*
" The author has made the incidents of every-day life a vehicle through which lessons of virtue, blended with religion, may be conveyed."—*Kilkenny Moderator.*
" A story of country life, written by one who knows well how to describe both cottage and hall life."—
" It bears the impress of truth and Nature's simplicity throughout."—*Illustrated News of the World.*

XIII.

In 3 vols., price 31s. 6d.

SYBIL GREY.

" Sybil Grey is a novel to be read by a mother to a daughter, or by a father to the loved circle at the domestic fireside."—*Paisley Herald.*

XIV.

In 2 vols., price 21s.

THE COUNT DE PERBRUCK.

By HENRY COOKE, Esq.

" A tale of the Vendean war, invested with a new interest. Mr. Cooke has done his part most successfully. His vivid, graphic colouring and well-chosen incidents prove him a master in the art of historical delineation."—*Guardian.*

"Of Mr. Cooke's share in the work we can speak with deserved approbation."—*Press.*

" It has the merit of keeping alive the excitement of the reader till the closing page."—*Morning Post.*

" This highly-interesting romance will find a place amongst the standard works of fiction."—*Family Herald.*

" This is an experiment, and a successful one."—*Atlas.*

XV.

In 3 vols., price 31s. 6d.

THE CAMPBELLS.

" The story is full of interest."—*Enquirer.*

XVI.

In 3 vols., price 31s. 6d.

EBB AND FLOW.

" It will amuse those who like to find something out of the usual even tenor of a novel; to such it can fairly be recommended."—*The Sun.*

XVII.

In 1 vol., price 7s. 6d.

MILLY WARRENER.

" A pleasant, unpretending story; it is a life-like story of a young country girl more refined than her station. There are little incidental sketches of country characters which are clever and spirited."—*Athenæum.*

XVIII.

In 3 vols., price 31s. 6d.

MASTER AND PUPIL.

By MRS. MACKENZIE DANIELS.

XIX.

In 1 vol., price 5s. (In November.)

SPIRITUALISM, AND THE AGE WE LIVE IN.

By CATHARINE CROWE,

Author of " The Night Side of Nature," "Ghost Stories," &c.

XX.

In 2 vols. post 8vo., price 21s.

MY FIRST TRAVELS;

Including Rides in the Pyrenees ; Scenes during an Inundation at Avignon ; Sketches in France and Savoy ; Visits to Convents and Houses of Charity, &c. &c.

By SELINA BUNBURY.

XXI.

In 1 vol. post 8vo., price 10s. 6d.

OUR PLAGUE SPOT:

In connection with our Polity and Usages as regards our Women, our Soldiery, and the Indian Empire.

XXII.

In 2 vols., price 21s.

AMERICAN PHOTOGRAPHS.

By the MISSES TURNBULL.

" It is exceedingly amusing, and marked by energy and power."
—*Globe.*

" Twenty-six thousand miles of travel, by two young ladies, in search of the new, the beautiful, and the instructive ! We do not know that a reader could desire more amusing *compagnons de voyage* than these two sprightly, intelligent, well-educated, and observant young Englishwomen."—*Morning Advertiser.*

" A number of amusing anecdotes give life and interest to the narrative."—*Brighton Examiner.*

" Very pleasant gossipping volumes."—*Critic.*

" These volumes are replete with lively, entertaining sketches of American manners and customs, sayings and doings."—*Naval and Military.*

" Contains much information respecting the manners and habits of our transatlantic cousins."—*Sun.*

" The narrative is evidently truthful, as it is clear and intelligible."—*Herald.*

XXIII.

In 1 vol., price 10s. 6d.

SUNDAY, THE REST OF LABOUR.

Dedicated to the Archbishop of Canterbury.

" This important subject is discussed ably and temperately ; and though many differences will arise in the minds of some of our clergy, as well as some pious laymen, it should be added to every library."—*Herald.*

" Written by a churchman, who is evidently a man with deep and sincere religious feelings. His book is temperately written, and will have a wholesome tendency, if wisely received."—*Eaminer.*

XXIV.

In 1 vol., price 2s. 6d.

DRAWING-ROOM CHARADES FOR ACTING.

By C. WARREN ADAMS, Esq.

" A valuable addition to Christmas diversions. It consists of a number of well-constructed scenes for charades."—*Guardian.*

XXV.

In 1 vol., price 12s.

MERRIE ENGLAND.

By LORD WILLIAM LENNOX.

" It overflows with racy, poignant anecdotes of a generation just passed away. The book is destined to lie upon the tables of many a country mansion."—*Leader.*

XXVI.

In 1 vol., price 5s.

KNIGHTS OF THE CROSS.

By MRS. AGAR.

" Nothing can be more appropriate than this little volume, from which the young will learn how their forefathers venerated and fought to preserve those places hallowed by the presence of the Saviour."—*Guardian.*

" Mrs Agar has written a book which young and old may read with profit and pleasure."—*Sunday Times.*

" It is a work of care and research, which parents may well wish to see in the hands of their children."—*Leader.*

" A well-written history of the Crusades, pleasant to read, and good to look upon."—*Critic.*

XXVII.

In 1 vol. post 8vo. price 10s. 6d.

AN AUTUMN IN SILESIA, AUSTRIA PROPER, AND THE OBER ENNS.

By the Author of " Travels in Bohemia."

XXVIII.

STEPS ON THE MOUNTAINS.

" This is a step in the right way, and ought to be in the hands of the youth of both sexes."—*Review.*

" The moral of this graceful and well-constructed little tale is, that Christian influence and good example have a better effect in doing the good work of reformatoin than the prison, the treadmill, or even the reformatory."—*Critic.*

"The Steps on the Mountains are traced in a loving spirit. They are earnest exhortations to the sober and religious-minded to undertake the spiritual and temporal improvement of the condition of the destitute of our lanes and alleys. The moral of the tale is well carried out; and the bread which was cast upon the waters is found after many days, to the saving and happiness of all therein concerned."—*Athenæum.*

XXIX.

In 1 vol., price 5s. •

FISHES AND FISHING.

By W. WRIGHT, Esq.

" Anglers will find it worth their while to profit by the author's experience."—*Athenæum.*

" The pages abound in a variety of interesting anecdotes connected with the rod and the line. The work will be found both useful and entertaining to the lovers of the piscatory art."—*Morning Post.*

" It is both amusing and instructive."—*Daily Telegraph.*

"A pleasant and gossipping book on the subject, with authentic facts gleaned from sources which could be depended upon, and worthy to be remembered, relative to angling in all its branches." —*Lancet.*

XXX.

DEAFNESS AND DISEASES OF THE EAR.

The Fallacies of the Treatment exposed, and Remedies suggested. From the Experience of half a Century.

By W. WRIGHT, Esq.,

Surgeon Aurist to her late Majesty, Queen Charlotte.

XXXI.

In 1 vol. post 8vo. 10s. 6d.

ZEAL IN THE WORK OF THE MINISTRY.

By L'ABBE DUBOIS.

"There is a tone of piety and reality in the work of l'Abbe Dubois, and a unity of aim, which is to fix the priest's mind on the duties and responsibilities of his whole position, and which we admire. The writer is occupied supremely with one thought of contributing to the salvation of souls and to the glory of God."— *Literary Churchman.*

XXXII.

In 1 vol., price 10s. 6d.

THE NEW EL DORADO; OR

BRITISH COLUMBIA.

By KINAHAN CORNWALLIS.

"The book is full of information as to the best modes existing or expected of reaching these enviable countries."— *Morning Chronicle.*

"The book gives all the information which it is possible to obtain respecting the new colony called British Columbia. The book is altogether one of a most interesting and instructive character." — *The Star.*

"The work is very spiritedly written, and will amuse and instruct."— *Observer.*

XXXIII.

In 2 vols. post 8vo., price 21s.

A PANORAMA OF THE NEW WORLD.

By KINAHAN CORNWALLIS,

Author of "Two Journeys to Japan," &c.

"Nothing can be more spirited, graphic, and full of interest, nothing more pictorial or brilliant in its execution and animation." — *Globe.*

"One of the most amusing tales ever written."— *Review.*

"He is a lively, rattling writer. The sketches of Peruvian Life and manners are fresh, racy and vigorous. The volumes abound with amusing anecdotes and conversations."— *Weekly Mail.*

XXXIV.

In 1 vol., price 10s. 6d.

NIL DESPERANDUM,

BEING AN ESCAPE FROM ITALIAN DUNGEONS.

" We find the volume entertaining, and really Italian in spirit."
—*Athenæum.*

" There is much fervour in this romantic narrative of suffering."
—*Examiner.*

XXXV.

In 1 vol. 8vo. price 10s. 6d.

LIFE OF ALEXANDER THE FIRST.

By IVAN GOLOVIN.

" It is a welcome contribution to Russian imperial biography."
—*Leader.*

"Mr. Golovin possesses fresher information, a fresher mind and manner applied to Russian affairs, than foreigners are likely to possess."—*Spectator.*

XXXVI.

In 2 vols., price 21s.

THIRTY-FIVE YEARS OF A DRAMATIC AUTHOR'S LIFE.

By EDWARD FITZBALL, Esq.

" We scarcely remember any biography so replete with anecdotes of the most agreeable description. Everybody in the theatrical world, and a great many out of it, figure in this admirable biography."—*Globe.*

"One of the most curious collections of histrionic incidents ever put together. Fitzball numbers his admirers not by hundreds and thousands, but by millions."—*Liverpool Albion.*

"A most wonderful book about all sorts of persons."—*Birmingham Journal.*

XXXVII.

In 1 vol., price 10s. 6d.

GHOST STORIES.

By CATHARINE CROWE,

Author of " Night Side of Nature."

"Mrs. Crowe's volume will delight the lovers of the supernatural, and their name is legion."—*Morning Post.*

"These Tales are calculated to excite all the feelings of awe, and we may say of terror, with which Ghost Stories have ever been read."—*Morning Advertiser.*

XXXVIII.

In 2 vols. post 8vo.

TEA TABLE TALK.

By MRS. MATHEWS.

" Livingstone's Africa, and Mrs. Mathews' Tea Table Talk will be the two most popular works of the season."—*Bicester Herald.*

" It is ordinary criticism to say of a good gossiping book, that it is a volume for the sea-side, or for the fireside, or wet weather, or for a sunny nook, or in a shady grove, or for after dinner over wine and walnuts. Now these lively, gossiping volumes will be found adapted to all these places, times, and circumstances. They are brimfull of anecdotes. There are pleasant little biographical sketches and ambitious essays."—*Athenæum.*

" The anecdotes are replete with point and novelty and truthfulness."—*Sporting Magazine.*

" No better praise can be given by us than to say, that we consider this work one of, if not the most agreeable books that has come under our notice."—*Guardian.*

" For Book Clubs and Reading Societies no work can be found that will prove more agreeable."—*Express.*

" The widow of the late, and the mother of the present Charles Mathews would, under any circumstances, command our respect, and if we could not conscientiously praise her work, we should be slow to condemn it. Happily, however, the volumes in question are so good, that in giving this our favourable notice we are only doing justice to the literary character of the writer; her anecdotes are replete with point and novelty and truthfulness that stamps hem genuine."—*Sporting Review.*

XXXIX.

In 2 vols., post 8vo., price 21s.

TWO JOURNEYS TO JAPAN.

By KINAHAN CORNWALLIS.

" The mystery of Japan melts away as we follow Mr. Cornwallis. He enjoyed most marvellous good fortune, for he carried a spell with him which dissipated Japanese suspicion and procured him all sorts of privileges. His knowledge of Japan is considerable. It is an amusing book."—*Athenæum.*

" This is an amusing book, pleasanly written, and evidencing generous feeling."—*Literary Gazette.*

" We can honestly recommend Mr. Cornwallis's book to our readers."—*Morning Herald.*

" The country under his pencil comes out fresh, dewy, and picturesque before the eye. The volumes are full of amusement, lively and graphic."—*Chambers' Journal.*

XL.

In 1 vol. post 8vo., price 10s. 6d.

HISTORICAL GLEANINGS
AT HOME AND ABROAD.
By MRS. JAMIESON.

"This work is characterized by forcible and correct descriptions of men and manners in bygone years. It is replete with passages of the deepest interest."—*Review*.

XLI.

In 1 vol., price 5s.

THINGS WORTH KNOWING ABOUT HORSES.
By HARRY HIEOVER.

"From the days of Nimrod until now no man has made so many, few more valuable additions to what may be called 'Sporting Literature.' To those skilled in horses this little volume will be very welcome, whilst to the raw youth its teachings will be as precious as refined gold."—*Critic*.

"Into this little volume Harry Hieover has contrived to cram an innumerable quantity of things worth knowing about the tricks and bad habits of all kinds of horses, harness, starting, shying and trotting; about driving; about the treatment of ailing horses; about corns, peculiarities of shape and make; and about stables, training, and general treatment."—*Field*.

"It is a useful hand-book about horses."—*Daily Telegraph*.

"Few men have produced better works upon the subject of horses than Harry Hieover."—*Review*.

"The author has omitted nothing of interest in his 'Things worth knowing about horses.'"—*Athenæum*.

XLII.

In 1 vol., demy 8vo., price 12s.

THE SPORTSMAN'S FRIEND IN A FROST.
By HARRY HIEOVER.

"Harry Hieover's practical knowledge and long experience in field sports, render his writings ever amusing and instructive. He relates most pleasing anecdotes of flood and field, and is well worthy of study."—*The Field*.

"No sportsman's library should be without it."—*Sporting Magazine*.

"There is amusement as well as intelligence in Harry Hieover's book."—*Athenæum*.

XLIII.

In 1 vol., price 5s.

THE SPORTING WORLD.

By HARRY HIEOVER.

"Reading Harry Hieover's book is like listening lazily and luxuriously after dinner to a quiet, gentlemanlike, clever talker."—*Athenæum.*

"It will be perused with pleasure by all who take an interest in the manly game of our fatherland. It ought to be added to every sportsman's library."—*Sporting Review.*

XLIV.

In 1 vol. demy 8vo., price 12s.

SPORTING FACTS AND SPORTING FANCIES.

By HARRY HIEOVER,

Author of "Stable Talk and Table Talk," "The Pocket and the Stud," "The Hunting Field," &c.

"This work will make a valuable and interesting addition to the Sportman's Library."—*Bell's Life.*

"In addition to the immense mass of practical and useful information with which this work abounds, there is a refreshing buoyancy and dash about the style, which makes it as attractive and fascinating as the pages of the renowned Nimrod himself."—*Dispatch.*

"It contains graphic sketches of celebrated young sporting characters."—*Sunday Times.*

XLV.

In 1 vol., price 5s. Third edition.

THE PROPER CONDITION FOR ALL HORSES.

By HARRY HIEOVER.

"It should be in the hands of all owners of horses."—*Bell's Life.*

"A work which every owner of a horse will do well to consult."—*Morning Herald.*

"Every man who is about purchasing a horse, whether it be hunter, riding-horse, lady's palfrey, or cart-horse, will do well to make himself acquainted with the contents of this book."—*Sporting Magazine.*

XLVI.

In 1 vol., price 5s. '

THE WORLD AND HOW TO SQUARE IT.

By HARRY HIEOVER.

XLVII.

In 1 vol., price 5s.

PRECEPT AND PRACTICE.

By HARRY HIEOVER.

XLVIII.

In 1 vol., price 5s.

HINTS TO HORSEMEN,

SHEWING HOW TO MAKE MONEY BY HORSES.

By HARRY HIEOVER.

"When Harry Hieover gives hints to Horsemen, he does not mean by that term riders exclusively, but owners, breeders, buyers, sellers, and admirers of horses. To teach such men how to make money is to impart no valueless instruction to a large class of mankind. The advice is frankly given, and if no benefit result, it will not be for the want of good counsel."—*Athenæum.*

"It is by far the most useful and practical book that Harry Hieover has written."—*Express.*

XLIX.

In 1 vol., price 4s.

BIPEDS AND QUADRUPEDS.

By HARRY HIEOVER.

"We recommend this little volume for the humanity towards quadrupeds it advocates, and the proper treatment of them that it inculcates."—*Bell's Life.*

L.

CHRISTMAS GIFT BOOK.

Price 1s. 6d.

PRINCE LIFE.

By G. P. R. JAMES, ESQ.,

Author of " The Gipsy," " Richelieu," &c.

" It is worth its weight in gold."—*The Globe.*

" Most valuable to the rising generation ; an invaluable little book."—*Guardian.*

LI.

In 2 vols. post 8vo., price 21s.

NAPLES,

POLITICAL, SOCIAL, AND RELIGIOUS.

By LORD B * * * * *

" The pictures are as lively and bright as the colours and climate they reflect."—*Spectator.*

" It is a rapid, clear historical sketch."—*Advertiser.*

"The author has done good service to society."—*Court Circular.*

LII.

In 2 vols., price 21s., cloth.

THE LIFE OF PERCY BYSSHE SHELLEY.

By CAPTAIN MEDWIN,

Author of " Conversations with Lord Byron."

" This book must be read by every one interested in literature." —*Morning Post.*

" A complete life of Shelley was a desideratum in literature, and there was no man so competent as Captain Medwin to supply it."—*Inquirer.*

" The book is sure of exciting much discussion."—*Literary Gazette.*

LIII.

Second Edition, now ready, in 3 vols., price 42s.

THE LITERARY LIFE AND CORRESPONDENCE

OF THE

COUNTESS OF BLESSINGTON.

By R. MADDEN, Esq., F.R.C.S.-ENG.

Author of " Travels in the East," " Life of Savonarola," &c.

" We may, with perfect truth affirm, that during the last fifty years there has been no book of such peculiar interest to the literary and political world. It has contributions from every person of literary reputation—Byron, Sir E. Bulwer, who contributes an original Poem) James, D'Israeli, Marryatt, Savage Landor, Campbell, L. E. L., the Smiths, Shelley, Jenkyn, Sir W. Gell, Jekyll, &c. &c.; as well as letters from the most eminent Statesmen and Foreigners of distinction, the Duke of Wellington, Marquis Wellesley, Marquis Douro, Lords Lyndhurst, Brougham, Durham, Abinger, &c."—*Morning Post.*

LIV.

Price 2s. 6d. beautifully illustrated.

THE HAPPY COTTAGE,

A TALE FOR SUMMER'S SUNSHINE.

By the Author of "Kate Vernon," "Agnes Waring."

LV.

In 1 vol., price 7s. 6d.

ON SEX IN THE WORLD TO COME.

By the Rev. G. B. HAUGHTON, A.M.

"A peculiar subject; but a subject of great interest, and in this volume treated in a masterly style. The language is surpassingly good, showing the author to be a learned and a thoughtful man."—*New Quarterly Review.*

LVI.

In 1 vol., 8vo.

THE AGE OF PITT AND FOX.

By DANIEL OWEN MADDEN,

Author of "Chiefs of Poarty," &c.

The *Times* says "We may safely pronounce it to be the best text-book of the age which it professes to describe."

LVII.

In 3 vols. demy 8vo., price 2l. 14s.

A CATHOLIC HISTORY OF ENGLAND.

By W. B. MAC CABE, Esq.

"A work of great literary value."—*Times.*

LVIII.

In 1 vol., price 14s.

LIVES OF THE PRIME MINISTERS OF ENGLAND.

FROM THE RESTORATION TO THE PRESENT TIME.

By J. HOUSTON BROWN, L.L.B.

Of the Inner Temple, Barrister-at-Law.

"The Biographer has collected the facts relating to the family and career of his four subjects, Clarendon, Clifford, Danby and Essex, and stated these facts with clearness;—selected such personal traits as the memoirs and lampoons of the time have presented, and interspersed his biographies with passing notices of the times and reflections, which though sometimes harsh in character or questionable in taste, have independence, and, at all events, a limited truth."—*Spectator.*

LIX.

In 2 vols. price 21s.

SHELLEY AND HIS WRITINGS.

By C. S. MIDDLETON, Esq.

" Never was there a more perfect specimen of biography."— *Walter Savage Landor, Esq.*

"Mr. Middleton has done good service. He has carefully sifted the sources of information we have mentioned, has made some slight addition, and arranged his materials in proper order and in graceful language. It is the first time the mass of scattered information has been collected, and the ground is therefore cleared for the new generation of readers."—*Athenæum.*

"The Life of the Poet which has just appeared, and which was much required, is written with great beauty of expression and clearness of purpose. Mr. Middleton's book is a masterly performance."—*Somerset Gazette.*

"Mr. Middleton has displayed great ability in following the poet through all the mazes of his life and thoughts. We recommend the work as lively, animated, and interesting. It contains many curious disclosures."—*Sunday Times.*

LX.

In 1 vol. price 10s. 6d.

THE HOME OF OUR PRINCESS;

OR, MOUNTAINS AND CITIES.

By SIBELLA JONES.

" The style is pleasing and tripping, the incidents striking and nnmerous, and the estimates of trans-Rhenan character free from educational bias and national prejudices."—*Daily Telegraph.*

LXI.

In 1 vol. 8vo. with Map.

THE HISTORY OF THE BERMUDAS.

By G. F. WILLIAMS, Esq.

LXI.

In 2 vols. post 8vo. price 21s.

THE AUSTRIAN EMPIRE.

By WILLIAM PEAKE, Esq.

"It has great historic value, and likely to be valuable for references."—*Daily News.*

"It presents by far the best view that has yet appeared of Austria."—*Naval and Military Gazette.*

LONDON: T. C. NEWBY, 30, WELBECK STREET,

CAVENDISH SQUARE.

www.ingramcontent.com/pod-product-compliance
Lightning Source LLC
Chambersburg PA
CBHW020859020726
47497CB00005B/1483